Exiled Sector World

Venom Island by Lexi C. Foss

Nightmare Island by Mila Young

Outcast Island by Jennifer Thorn

Other Standalone Stories in this World:
X-Clan Series

X-Clan: The Origin

Andorra Sector

X-Clan: The Experiment

Winter's Arrow

Bariloche Sector

V-Clan Series

Blood Sector

Night Sector

Eclipse Sector

LEXI C. FOSS

Venom ISLAND

~ AN EXILED SECTOR NOVEL ~

This is a work of fiction. Names, characters, places, and incidents are either the product of the author's imagination or are used fictitiously, and any resemblance to actual persons, living or dead, business establishments, events, or locales is entirely coincidental.

Venom Island

Editing by: Outthink Editing, LLC

Proofreading by: Katie Schmahl & Jean Bachen

Cover Design: Covers by Juan

Cover Photography: Wander Aguiar

Cover Models: Vargo & Kiana

Map Illustration: Ricky Gunawan

Title Page & Chapter Art: Covers by Julie

Published by: Ninja Newt Publishing, LLC

Digital Edition

ISBN: 978-1-68530-252-8

Print Edition

ISBN: 978-1-68530-362-4

AI Disclaimer: This book does not contain any elements of AI content. All art was designed by real artists, and all of the words were written by the author.

For those who enjoy quick, knotty reads with satisfying happily-ever-after endings.

Enrique is ready to make you purr, little treasure…

ABOUT VENOM ISLAND

Welcome to the Exiled Sector, home to the most lethal Alphas on the planet.
These beings don't play nice with others.
They've been banished.
And a plane full of Omegas just crash-landed on their isles.

We're being hunted.
Their feral growls follow us.
Their howls haunt us.
Their knots call to us.
And their savagery terrifies us.

Some will escape.
Some will be caught.
Three will be *claimed*.

My name is Caja. And this is the story of how an Alpha named Enrique saved me from the horrors of Bariloche Sector.

Only to end up crash-landing our plane on Venom Island…

WELCOME TO EXILED SECTOR...
HOME TO THE MOST LETHAL ALPHAS ON THE PLANET.

THESE BEINGS DON'T PLAY NICE WITH OTHERS. THEY'VE BEEN BANISHED.
AND A PLANE FULL OF OMEGAS JUST CRASH-LANDED ON THEIR ISLES.

This world isn't kind. It's futuristic and dystopian, and over 90 percent of the human population no longer exists. Supernaturals are in charge here, their territories often referred to as "sectors," where Alphas make the rules and everyone else obeys. Those who don't are either killed or sent to Exiled Sector.

Venom Island.
Nightmare Island.
Outcast Island.

All of these islands are part of the notorious Exiled Sector. They're all governed and ruled in entirely different ways. The supernatural species and their dynamics may vary. And they manage themselves.

There's only one rule that applies to all of Exiled Sector: Once you've been marked for exile, there's no going back. Exiled Sector is your home now. Embrace it. Survive it. Or die.

Alpha Enrique and Omega Caja are the main characters of *Venom Island*, a place where chaos reigns. It's a jungle filled with deadly beings, and it's in desperate need of a regime change.

Below are some themes you may find in *Venom Island*:
✔ Consent Between Hero and Heroine
✔ Mentions of Nonconsent/Rape to Tertiary Characters
✔ Uncomfortable Upbringing for Heroine (Forced Starvation/Dehydration, Captivity, Abusive Father Figure)
✔ No Other Woman or Other Man Drama (No Cheating)
✔ Pregnancy/Breeding
✔ Primal Energy
✔ Possessive Over The Top Alpha Male
✔ Touch Her and Die Vibes
✔ Knotting, Nesting, Purring, Growling (I mean, obviously the book wouldn't be complete without these things, right?)

VENOM ISLAND

OUTCAST ISLAND

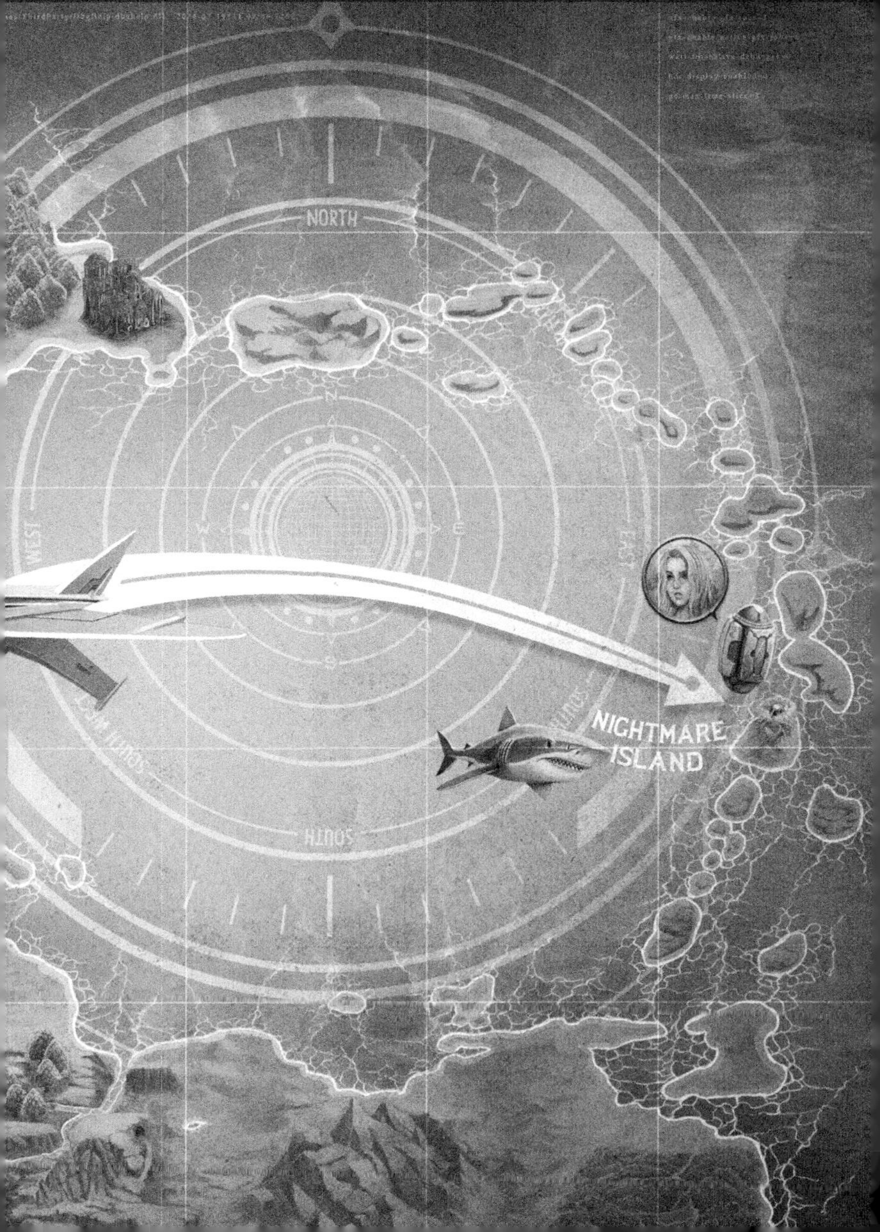
NORTH
WEST
EAST
SOUTH
NIGHTMARE ISLAND

CAJA

A LOUD CRACK SHAKES THE FOUNDATION OF MY CAGE, causing the hairs along my arms to dance.

Whimpers sound all around me.

Sobs, too.

I'm new to this hell, yet I've known it would be my fate all my life. My Alpha—the one whose seed gave me life—told me of my destiny long, long ago.

"Once you're of age, you're going to Alpha Carlos's playground," he spat at me, disgusted by my very existence.

I was an Omega. Useless. Only worth whatever price the Bariloche Sector Alpha was willing to pay for my existence.

It turns out that price wasn't much, hence the bruise marring my jaw.

"I should have killed you when you were a pup," my Alpha snarled before shoving me into this cage.

How many days ago was that? I wonder, my arms curling around my abdomen as I fight the shivers

1

traversing my bare spine. *When did I last eat or drink anything?*

Time is elusive here. A taunt. A way to enforce obedience and terrify the inhabitants of this underground prison.

I swallow as another shudder rattles my cage. I don't know what's coming, but it's intense.

"What is that?" one of the nearby Omegas asks, her voice just above a whisper.

"I don't know," another replies, her accent thick and foreign to my wolf ears.

I tuck my knees even tighter into my chest, my spine against the crisscrossed bars at my back. I can't stand in my cage, only kneel, which I choose not to do because the metal bottom digs into my exposed skin.

Another tremble vibrates my being as the booms grow louder and more powerful.

Inside, my animal whines, terrified of what's happening. Outwardly, I control my breathing and try to regulate my heartbeat.

My Alpha taught me to be quiet and motionless. He hated my voice. Loathed any sounds I made at all.

"The only thing an Omega is good for is taking a knot," he would say. "And I can't fucking knot you. So be thankful I let you breathe at all."

I was his only female child; all the others were males who felt the same way as my Alpha.

"Useless," they told me every day.

Because nothing I did was ever right. They hated my cooking. Hated my cleaning. Hated my very existence.

And so did the other Omegas.

"You have no reason to cry," my caregiver—an Omega who wasn't my mother but the female my Alpha put in charge of my upbringing—once snapped. "They never touch you, and they'll never knot you. So just do your damn job, Caja, and clean up this mess."

I think I was eight then. Maybe nine?

At least a decade ago, I marvel. Because it felt like a hundred years ago.

Thunder reverberates around me, nearly causing my heart to jump out of my chest. But I quickly school my features, determined to face whatever is coming with a calm facade.

It's the best way to avoid punishment, I remind myself. *Just accept fate. Be quiet. And disappear into the background.*

Only that becomes harder and harder to do as the rumbling grows louder with each passing second. Until suddenly, silence falls entirely.

I stop breathing, my ears straining to pick up on any subtle shifts in the air, any undercurrent of danger.

Nothing.

I exhale.

Inhale.

Listen again.

Still quiet.

But a burning scent trickles into the air, causing my nose to wrinkle in response.

Someone whimpers again in the room.

Another whine.

And smoke starts to thicken around us.

Followed by the faint echo of crackling.

A fire, I realize, my calm facade slipping as my heart

3

kicks off into a chaotic rhythm in my chest. *Something's on fire. And I'm trapped in a cage.*

Oh, moons...

I press my palm to the metal, my fingers only partially able to slide through the holes in the crisscrossed pattern. I haven't tried escaping or moving much at all since my Alpha unceremoniously dumped me here. There wasn't a point. If I ran, I would be hunted, rutted, and potentially killed. That was what happened to Omegas in my home pack.

I have every reason to believe the same will happen here.

But I don't want to be *burned* to death.

I push against the metal, my fear rising as the acrid stench grows stronger and stronger. Just like the flickering crinkle of an approaching flame.

Shit, shit, shit...

The cage won't budge.

Stealing a deep breath—and wincing as the smoke infiltrates my lungs—I study the edges of the cage, then the place where my Alpha locked me inside.

Is there a way to—

Pounding fills my ears in the next instant, the reverberation of Alpha growls adding a deep base to the otherwise ominous soundtrack.

I freeze, then jolt backward to hold my knees against my bare chest once more, determined to represent the epitome of submission.

A door slams open, sending a jitter down my spine that I try to fight. But my pulse betrays me, my heart beating a little too fast.

"*Fuck*," an Alpha snarls. "Enrique! Elias! There are more down here!"

My ears prick upward as harsh footsteps follow the male's shouting.

"They're in fucking cages!" the Alpha adds, sounding livid.

I curl into myself as tight as I can, not wanting to be on the receiving end of that fury. Because he sounds like he wants to kill everyone in sight. And I know all too well what Alphas do when furious.

He skips my cage, going toward the back of the room.

My shoulders fall a bit, temporary relief allowing my nerves to calm. Only for the hairs along my arms to stand on end once more as two burly shadows enter the space.

"Shit," one of them says. "This must be a new shipment."

"New shipment?" the third repeats.

"Yeah," he grouses, his irritation seeming to pour off of him in waves. "Alphas from all over the world trade their Omegas to Carlos for all sorts of shit—used Omega toys, serums, drugs, psychedelics, you name it."

The third Alpha snorts. "Makes me wish he could die again."

"If only," the Alpha drawls, his focus shifting my way. "I've got this one."

My heart stops, as does my breathing. *The irritated one is coming for me. He's going to—*

"Shh," he hushes, a strange rumble igniting in his chest as he approaches my cage.

I cock my head, confused by the foreign vibration. It's a very curious growl. Or maybe... maybe not a growl at all.

"I'm not going to hurt you, little one," he tells me before ripping the lock off my cage door—the action betraying his true intentions.

I can't help pressing back into the wires behind me, my body instantly on high alert.

But he doesn't try to yank me out of the crate. Instead, he holds out a hand, his voice lowering as he murmurs, "Come on out, sweetheart. We need to go outside, then we'll get you somewhere safe."

Safe? I repeat in my head. *Nowhere is safe.*

This world was overrun by a zombielike plague, killing most of humankind and leaving several supernaturals dead as well.

Not my kind, though.

X-Clan wolves are immune. Some others are, too.

But we're controlled by Alphas. And Alphas are the epitome of danger.

There is no such concept as *safe*.

"Please?" he asks, the word one I don't think I've ever heard used in my presence. I know what it means because I often utter it when requesting food or water. But for an Alpha to say it? To me?

How utterly bizarre.

Several other cages rattle as Omegas are freed one by one, the other Alphas saying similar things to them as this one has said to me.

"Up the stairs," the third Alpha says to a pair of

shivering females. "Sven and Kazek will show you where to go."

The Omegas scatter, not bothering to question the Alpha's words or even hesitate before following his command.

Yet I sit here very much questioning the male in front of me.

He crouches a little, his face shrouded in darkness. However, a hint of yellow flashes at me as his wolf stares me down. "I'm not going to hurt you," he repeats, but in Spanish this time. "You can trust me."

I frown, confused by his shift in languages.

When I don't respond, he says something else, only this time I don't understand what he's saying at all, as it's all gibberish.

He tries once more, his sounds more guttural and harsher in nature.

"Russian, maybe?" the third Alpha suggests as he comes to stand by my cage.

"I don't know Russian. Only English, Spanish, Italian, and German."

"Hmm," the male hums, bending to peer into my cage.

I flinch away from him, more afraid of him than the other male. I'm not sure why, but the one who spoke all the languages just seems less intimidating.

"We're not going to hurt you," the third Alpha says, speaking English. "I'm Elias. If you scent me, you'll know I'm already mated."

I'm not sure why that matters, so I just stare at him.

"This is Enrique. He's not mated, but he believes in

7

consent." The third Alpha—*Elias*—glances at his friend. "Right?"

"Yes," the less intimidating one says but doesn't elaborate.

"We're here to burn this hellhole to the ground. But to do that, I need you to leave that cage and go upstairs," Elias tells me.

I blink at him. *Burn it to the ground? Is that why I'm smelling fire?*

Enrique repeats what Elias said, only in Spanish, then switches to the other languages he knows.

"I understand English," I finally tell him. "And Spanish."

He says nothing for a long moment, his gaze seeming to search mine despite the darkness around us. Perhaps his wolf sight is better than mine because all I see are the shadows of his face, but I can feel the intensity of his eyes.

He holds out his hand for me again, his arm having dropped when Elias joined him at the cage. "Will you please come upstairs with me?" he asks in Spanish rather than English.

I swallow. It's akin to suicide to deny an Alpha. I'm not sure why I haven't obeyed him yet. It was purely instinctual not to, which is strange given how often I've followed Alpha orders over the years.

Clearing my throat, I finally push forward, but slowly because of the tight space.

Enrique takes a step backward, his hand still poised in offering as I reach the open door.

I glance from him to the floor, trying to determine

the best way to get down, as my cage is perched on a table. If I were in wolf form, I would simply jump. But on two legs—and without the appropriate room to stand —I'm more likely to fall flat on my face from here.

Being hungry and thirsty isn't helping matters, either.

Closing my eyes, I blow out a breath and finally place my hand in Enrique's large palm. Electricity hums up my arm in response to the simple touch. That electric current only grows stronger as he gently pulls me out of the cage and into his arms before setting me on my feet.

I wobble, my legs and back sore from being bent for so long. Wincing, I try to step forward, only to lose my balance entirely and end up tucked against a big Alpha chest.

That vibration sound he made earlier rumbles back to life, stirring a quivering sensation in my lower belly. *That's a very pleasing growl*, I decide.

It makes me want to melt into his broad chest and nuzzle his pecs.

"I've never heard an Alpha do this," I confide softly as he starts carrying me up the stairs. "What is it?"

He stills on the steps, the abrupt halt making me realize my faux pas.

I just questioned an Alpha.

Oh, what in the moons was I thinking?

"I'm sorry, Alpha," I immediately add, my head bowing as much as I can in my position against his torso. "I… I won't speak again."

"You can speak however much you like," he replies,

that vibration heightening with his words. "And it's a purr, pequeño tesoro."

Little treasure, I translate, shivering. That seems like an abnormal thing to call me. Perhaps I misheard him?

He starts up the stairs once more, not saying anything else.

I remain quiet as well, then flinch as light hits my eyes from above. It's blinding. Too bright. *Overwhelming.* And it makes it impossible for me to see what we're doing. Not that I have any choice in where we're going or what will happen once we get there.

"She's underfed but otherwise appears to be unhurt," I hear him say.

"All right. Take her to the tree line," a deep voice replies. *Another Alpha.* "We've set up a few blankets with food and water. She'll need to be on one of the later flights."

"Will do," Enrique replies, the world moving as he starts walking.

It isn't until the scent of forest hits me that my eyesight begins to recover, and by then, Enrique is setting me down on something soft.

"Try to eat," he tells me. "Ander will be by soon with an update on what happens next."

That sounds foreboding, I think, but just nod in response. Mostly because I don't know what else to say or do.

His knuckles brush against my cheek, drawing my gaze up to his face, causing my breath to catch in my throat.

Because *wow*.

Tall. Broad-shouldered. Sexy fucking Alpha.

And his eyes are a beautiful shade of black that reminds me of the night.

I've never seen an Alpha like this. No scars. No harsh lines. No unkempt hair or spittle running down his chin.

Just perfectly chiseled features. *And dimples*, I think as his full lips turn upward a little. "Hi, little wolf." His knuckles brush my cheek again just as someone calls his name from behind him. "Eat, pequeño tesoro. One of us will be back soon to check on you."

He stands, making me realize he was crouching by the blanket before. Now that he's at full height, I can't help gaping up at him. He's positively massive. If I stood beside him, the top of my head might reach his chest.

Yet I'm not scared of him.

Maybe because of the way he looks at me, or perhaps it's his tone. *Or that purr*, I think as he walks away. My gaze drops to his backside, my cheeks warming as I admire his firm ass in those tight jeans.

I don't think I've ever ogled an Alpha before, but this one... this one is worthy of admiration.

"Do you want a blanket?" someone whispers beside me, reminding me that I'm not alone out here. Part of me already knew that, mostly because my nose notified me of the other scents. But my focus was entirely on Enrique before.

Now I glance at the three other Omegas huddling by the food, their eyes wide as they stare at me.

A blonde with long braids holds something toward

me, suggesting she's the one who asked me about a blanket.

I nod and take it, wrapping the fabric around my bare skin. I've been without clothes for so long that I hardly register the warmth the blanket brings. Every part of me is cold.

Or, at least, every part of me *was* cold.

My side is warm.

The side that was against Alpha Enrique's chest moments ago.

It's almost as though his natural heat had bled into my skin, marking me as his.

I rather like that thought.

"They're grouping us together in different shipments," the Omega with the braids informs me. "None of us know where we're going."

I look at her again, noting her blue eyes and pale skin. Very different from my dark hair, black eyes, and tan complexion. The shape of her eyes is different, too. Unique. I've never seen anyone with her features. Nor have I ever smelled a wolf like her.

Not an X-Clan wolf, I decide.

The female beside her isn't one either.

Actually, I don't think the woman beside her is a wolf at all.

"What are you?" I wonder out loud, my gaze on the blondish-brown-haired being of unknown descent.

She blinks a pair of startling red eyes at me, glances at the others, and then returns her focus to me once more. "Um. I'm a vampire."

My gaze widens. "Oh." That's… that's interesting. "And you?" I ask the one with long braids.

"Ulv wolf," she tells me.

"I see. I'm an X-Clan wolf," I say, earning a nod from the third Omega, who I can tell is the same type as me because of her scent.

"What's your name?" the Ulv wolf asks.

"Caja," I tell her. "You?"

"Hel," she replies, then gestures to the vampire as she adds, "This is Guðrún. We just met."

"And I'm Paige," the X-Clan wolf says before Hel can introduce her. "I've only been here for a few days."

"Same," Hel echoes.

"Me, too," Guðrún murmurs.

Perhaps that's why we're all grouped together— we're the *new shipment*, as Enrique said a bit ago.

"Hopefully, we won't be staying for much longer," I say, my gaze finding the Alpha in question across an open green space. He stands with his arms folded over his broad chest, his gaze on two Alphas of similar size and stature.

"Are they taking us somewhere worse?" the vampire asks in a low whisper.

"I don't know," Hel replies. "But I think we're going to find out soon."

ENRIQUE

I can feel the Omega's eyes on me from across the field, her dark orbs resembling a brand against my skin.

Stunning, I think, picturing her gaze with ease. *Absolutely stunning.*

And naked.

So fucking naked.

Gods, it took restraint to keep my focus on her face. It was so damn wrong. She was vulnerable. Clearly abused. *A captive.*

And without a doubt, the most beautiful Omega I've ever seen.

"I've given the others clearance to land," Ander is saying, his dominant aura ensuring all of us are listening. "Once we do, we'll load up the injured Omegas that require the most medical intervention and send them to Andorra Sector. Riley's already prepping for their arrival."

I nod. Riley's an Omega and a doctor. I've only

spent a few minutes with the little blue-haired spitfire, but she's a force of nature.

"What about those who don't require immediate medical attention?" Kaz asks, his dominance rivaling Ander's. They're both X-Clan Sector Alphas. However, Ander is the more experienced of the two.

While their domineering auras agitate my inner wolf, I wouldn't want to challenge either of them. Not because I fear them, necessarily. I just respect them too damn much to try to fight them.

Besides, I owe them both a debt of gratitude for allowing me to accompany them on this mission.

Not only did I have a past to face here in Bariloche Sector, but I had a brother to save.

A twin who's currently being detained on one of the jets, I think, wincing. *At least he's alive.*

Although, after seeing him in that cage an hour ago, I'm not quite sure Joseph *wants* to be alive.

"The X-Clan Omegas who can heal on their own don't need to go to Andorra Sector," Ander says, addressing Kaz's question regarding the healthier Omegas. "In fact, I would prefer them to go elsewhere. It'll make this less complicated. Can you take any in Winter Sector?"

"If they're willing, yes," Kaz replies.

Ander nods. "We can give them a choice—Andorra Sector, Winter Sector, or Norse Sector. Because they can't stay here."

"What about the Omegas who aren't X-Clan wolves?" I wonder out loud, glancing back at the group where I left my little Omega treasure.

"We'll need to reach out to some allies to provide them with options," Ander replies.

Kaz grunts. "Good luck finding a vampire ally."

I snort, agreeing with him.

Vampire Alphas are fucking terrifying.

"Too bad Kieran didn't stick around to help with that one," Kaz adds.

"Or anything else," Sven mutters as he joins our little circle. He looks nothing like his brother, Ander. Sven is blond with light eyes, while Ander has dark hair and golden eyes. Sven also appears to be a bit less dominant than his older brother, yet no less intimidating.

Elias is the last one to round out our group, the five of us having led the attack against the former Alpha of Bariloche Sector.

Well, technically, we had help from a few V-Clan wolves.

But Kieran and his two Elites fucked off the moment they found what they wanted in Carlos's estate, leaving the rest of us to clean up the mess.

I suppose it's only fair. This is X-Clan territory, after all. And most of the Omegas in Carlos's dungeons were of X-Clan origin.

Including my little treasure, I think, looking at her once more.

This time, I catch her staring at me, her almond-shaped eyes striking even from a distance.

Ander and Sven begin discussing flight logistics, talking about who will be going where, while I hold the pretty Omega's gaze. It takes her a few beats to lower her eyes, causing my wolf to stir inside me. We like strong Omegas, ones who are not afraid to challenge our authority.

Upon first meeting, I would say this one isn't the type to challenge me at all.

But now… now I'm not so sure.

"All right, that just leaves us with the uninjured, non-X-Clan Omegas," Ander says, drawing my focus back to him. Because now he's talking about my little treasure's group.

Although, she's an X-Clan Omega.

Which means he'll be offering her a pick of sectors.

I wonder where she'll prefer to go? I muse. *Where is she even from?*

Because she's not a Bariloche Sector Omega. I would recognize her if she were, since I grew up here.

"I'll start making calls, but I need some details, like names, how they ended up here, and if they have any preferences on where to go," Ander goes on. "Elias?"

"On it," the Andorra Sector's second-in-command drawls.

"I'll help," I offer, wanting something to do that doesn't involve thinking about my brother and his catatonic mate.

"You don't want to accompany your twin back to Andorra Sector?" Ander asks, arching a dark brow. "He'll be on the first flight out, which is leaving in ten minutes."

They knocked my brother out with some hefty tranquilizers after we found him in a rabid state inside

17

his cell. Unfortunately, those drugs won't last long. And my brother needs immediate treatment.

Just like a handful of other Alphas who'd been imprisoned with my brother, and several badly injured Omegas—including my twin's mate, Savi.

Ander put the Alphas on one and the Omegas on the other, wisely keeping them separated in case any of the feral Alphas escaped their restraints.

I swallow. "Do you need me to go with my brother? Or could you use my help here?" I ask, holding Ander's gaze. "I owe you a debt for helping to clean up this mess. And it feels wrong to leave in the middle of the process, especially when my familiarity with Bariloche Sector might still prove useful. But if you need more muscle on the jet carrying my twin, that's where I'll go."

The Andorra Sector Alpha considers me for a long moment. "You're right. You're more valuable here. But I'll understand if you need to accompany your brother." He glances at Sven before returning his focus to me. "It's what I would be tempted to do in your situation."

I run my fingers through my hair, my gaze flicking around the field and all the various groups of Omegas. "There's not much I can do for my brother at the moment. We found him. Now he needs medical intervention."

Assuming that will even be able to help him.

His snarling face populates my mind, making me wince deep within.

Joseph didn't recognize me at all. Hell, I wasn't even sure he knew his own name anymore, let alone mine.

I shake my head, clearing it. "There's not much I

can do for him on that jet other than knock him back out… which I really don't want to do."

Ander nods, understanding flashing in his golden eyes. "Then you'll help here. Besides, it'll be useful having another pilot on standby should we need one."

Elias claps his hand on my shoulder. "Let's start with Carlos's newest 'shipment,'" he says, referring to the last group we found in Carlos's underground bunkers. "They should be the easiest to question in terms of their history and how they arrived here. Then we'll work backward from there."

My gaze instantly goes to the little treasure wrapped up in a blanket. "Sounds good to me."

I let Elias take the lead, aware that the Omegas will be more comfortable with him due to his status as a mated Alpha.

Of course, being mated means little in Bariloche Sector, thanks to Carlos's former policies. He actively advocated the sharing of mated Omegas, primarily to punish the Alphas who claimed them.

The Alphas under his command, anyway.

Alphas like my brother.

The only way to break a bond between X-Clan mates was to kill the Alpha. Alas, the Omega often went insane as a result.

So Carlos chose to hold the Alphas in his dungeons while exploiting their Omega mates.

It was sick and twisted and fucking wrong. Being part of the team to take him down did little to assuage my guilt of my association with the bastard.

Most X-Clan sectors saw me as Bariloche Sector's

second-in-command, similar to Elias being Ander's Second in Andorra Sector. It wasn't my real title, as Carlos refused to name a Second. He considered me a general.

Alas, that distinction wouldn't matter to most of my kind. The affiliation and notoriety were very much there, and absolutely tainted my identity in our world.

Word would soon spread of my involvement in today's events, how I helped two other Sector Alpha's take down Carlos.

I have no idea what that means for my reputation, or where I'll even be welcome to live.

As it stands right now, I have no home. Mainly because I just helped Ander and Elias burn it to the ground.

I fight the urge to shuffle my feet, instead choosing to listen as Elias introduces himself—and me—to the group of Omegas huddled with my little tesoro.

She's the only one without clothes, suggesting she was delivered to Carlos in that state.

"Can you share your name, please? As well as what sector you're from?" Elias continues, his voice gentle as he takes a knee before the four Omegas.

Rather than kneel or squat behind him, I go and sit next to the Omega I carried out of the bunker.

She glances at me but doesn't try to move away, just watches as I extend my legs and cross them at the ankles. Resting my palms behind me on the ground, I lean back and meet her curious stare.

She shivers, causing me to reach out and more firmly wrap the blanket around her svelte form. It's such a natural response, one I realize might be intrusive a second too late.

But she doesn't seem bothered by it. Actually, her lips tilt a little upward in response, suggesting the opposite.

When Elias is done with his questions, I'll find her something to wear. She has to be cold. It might be summer in this part of the world, but it's still chilly in the mountains.

"I'm Paige," a petite X-Clan Omega says, her eyes lowered in deference. "I'm from Cusco Sector."

"Guðrún," the vampire beside her adds, her voice holding a tentative note to it. "Älva Nest." She doesn't look down like Paige does but instead stares at Elias cautiously, like she's waiting for him to comment further.

He simply nods and looks at the female with Nordic features. She's either an Ash wolf or an Ulv wolf, based on her scent. Her expression is borderline defiant as she introduces herself as "Hel."

"And where are you from, Hel?" Elias presses.

"That depends," she replies. "Why do you want to know?"

Elias considers her for a moment, his lips twitching despite her blatant rudeness.

Most Omegas bow to Alphas.

This one clearly does not.

Fortunately for her, Elias is pretty laid-back. I am, too.

If she attempts to speak to Ander or Kaz in this way, though, she will quickly be educated on X-Clan

21

hierarchy and what it means to be an Omega in our world.

"We're trying to determine where you came from and where you would like to go from here," Elias informs her, his tone underlined with patience. "You're welcome to join us in Andorra Sector, but we can also take you home, if that's your preference."

Hel narrows her gaze, suspicion clear in her expression. "That sounds too good to be true. And in my experience, *good* doesn't really exist in this world."

Guðrún nods in agreement, as does Paige.

But the Omega beside me stays quiet, her focus shifting from me to Elias.

"How did you end up here?" he asks, his attention on Hel. "Were you taken or traded?"

"Both," she growls. "Taken as an unwilling bride, then traded for a more submissive model." She folds her arms, her air of defiance returning with a vengeance. "Do you know Jarl?"

Elias frowns, glancing at me.

"I've never met anyone by that name," I tell him.

"Same," Elias says. "Who's Jarl?"

Hel stares at him for a long moment, evaluating him and then me. "He's a Balor wolf. From Wildborn Sector."

Elias's brow furrows even more.

But a bell goes off in my head, a face appearing in my memories. "Tall, crooked nose, pointy jaw, thinning blond hair? Smells like mold?"

Hel freezes, telling me I've not only described him

appropriately, but she's not his biggest fan. "You do know him."

"I've seen him around here a few times," I admit. "But no, I don't know him. He's also dead. One of the many Alpha casualties sustained today during our raid." I shrug. "I hope he didn't mean much to you." Because I can't exactly apologize for the loss. He, like many of the others, deserved his fate today.

"He… he's dead?" she repeats, her bravado seeming to fail her. "Oh." Her brow crinkles. "*Oh.*"

"Raid?" Paige asks, her gaze finally lifting from the ground. "W-what do you mean?"

"We've shut down Carlos's operations here," Elias tells her. "Now we have the very difficult task of returning you all to your homes, if that's where you want to go. So I'm going to ask again, where are you from? And if you don't want to share that, then where would you like to go?"

Hel and Paige look at each other, then Hel clears her throat.

"Savage Sector," she says. "My brother is Alpha Ragnar."

Elias's eyebrows lift a little in surprise, but he quickly masks it with a nod. "I don't know if we have open connections with him, but Ander has a contact in that region—Shadowland Sector—that he can lean on. We'll make it happen."

He looks at Paige. "I… I don't want to go back to Cusco Sector."

Not a surprising response. Cusco Sector isn't much better than Bariloche Sector.

"As I said, you're welcome in Andorra Sector. We also have Alphas in Norse Sector and Winter Sector who would be willing to take you in, if you prefer," Elias tells her before looking at Guðrún.

She says nothing for a long moment, then quietly tells him, "There's no place that's safe for a Vampire Omega."

"Maybe Kieran can help with this one?" I suggest.

Elias grimaces but concedes with a muttered "Maybe."

V-Clan wolves are similar to vampires in that they need to drink blood and prefer the night. Vampire Omegas are also compatible with V-Clan Alphas. So there's that benefit as well.

But yeah, I very much understand Elias's reluctance to reach out to Kieran. The V-Clan Alphas are exceptionally powerful, almost frighteningly so.

"What about you?" Elias asks, his attention falling on my silent little treasure.

She's been quietly observing the whole conversation, her beautiful black eyes glittering with intelligence. When I found her in that cage, I mistook her for being meek. But she's not. She's calm, collected, and very aware.

"My name is Caja," she says. "I've always been destined for Bariloche Sector, so I'm not sure where else to go."

"What do you mean, you were always destined for Bariloche Sector?" I ask her before Elias has a chance to respond. *This little treasure is mine*, I think, my wolf growling inside me in agreement.

Elias isn't a threat.

I know that.

But I don't want him questioning this Omega.

She's mine to question. Mine to protect. Just... *mine.*

I don't care if we just met. Her scent calls to me. Her beauty. *Her eyes.*

Eyes that remind me of black fire as she gazes up at me now. "My Alpha always said I would end up here. That's been my primary purpose since birth—to be traded once I came of age."

My jaw clenches, the notion that this beautiful Omega was only worth her value as a Bariloche Sector trade grating on my nerves. "What sector is your Alpha from?" I ask, doing my best to soften my tone and swallow my mounting rage.

She starts to reply, then stops and asks, "Will I go back there?"

"No," I answer immediately. *But I may visit and kill your Alpha*, I think darkly.

"Oh. Then... then does it matter?"

"Yes," I say without hesitation. Because the more I'm thinking about it, the more I want to destroy whoever dared to trade away this gorgeous little treasure. "Who gave you to Carlos?"

Her full bottom lip disappears between her teeth as she considers how to reply. "Alpha Bautista."

My wolf snarls inside, echoing the fury simmering through my veins.

Because I was wrong.

This female is from Bariloche Sector.

25

Perhaps not from the central part of the territory, but the outskirt lands under Carlos's former protection.

Bautista is—*was*—a sadistic asshole who lived about a hundred miles from here in a run-down village where he managed distribution for Carlos's Omega slave trade.

If this female was one Bautista felt he could barter for himself, that meant she was his daughter.

Fuck.

"Bautista's dead," I tell her.

And I'm the one that put a bullet through his head.

CAJA

I stare at the handsome Alpha, his words ringing through my thoughts.

Bautista's dead.

"You're sure?" I ask, my voice not giving away the chaos unfolding inside me. Because I have no idea what this means for me. Or where I'm to go next. Another sector? To a new Alpha?

Can I go with this one? I wonder, then wince internally at the idea.

I don't even know him.

But I… I kind of want *to know him.*

"Yes," he says, confusing me for half a beat before I recall the question I asked about him being certain that Alpha Bautista is dead. "I shot him," Enrique adds, swallowing. "He was helping to guard Carlos, and…" He shrugs, somehow looking both apologetic and unrepentant at the same time.

"Oh." My nose wrinkles. "I didn't realize he was still

27

here." I assumed he left me in that cage and returned to our pack.

But no.

He stayed.

And now he's dead.

"Oh," I repeat, blinking. I really don't know how to feel about this information. I honestly... don't feel much at all.

Elias clears his throat. "You don't need to decide where you want to go right now," he tells me. "But I will need an answer soon."

I glance at the other Alpha and nod. "Okay." Although, I have no idea what decision he expects me to make. I know nothing about the sectors he mentioned. My entire world is Bariloche Sector. My Alpha. And Alpha Carlos.

Who will I be now?

"All right, we have to go to the next group, but if you need anything, just call for us," Elias says as he stands once more. "We'll be back for your final decisions."

Hel and Guðrún nod.

I just stare at Enrique, already missing him despite the fact that he hasn't moved yet. *Is this strange fascination a result of him freeing me from my cage or something else?* I wonder, taking in his handsome features once more. *Why am I so enamored with this Alpha? Is it his perfect features? His kind eyes?*

"What would you like to wear?" he asks me instead of standing like the other Alpha. "Sweater? Jeans? A dress?"

My eyelashes flutter, confusion clouding my

thoughts. "I… I don't own any clothes." My Alpha made that very clear when he forced me to strip before getting in the cage.

"Those are mine," he sneered. *"Take them off."*

I shiver now, recalling the way his eyes tracked over me after I disrobed. Disgust and hate radiated from his dark eyes—so similar to my own.

"I should have killed you when you were a pup."

Then he shoved me into the crate.

And left.

"Caja," Enrique murmurs, drawing my attention to his mouth. "What do you usually wear back home?"

"Whatever my caretaker gives me," I tell him, blinking before raising my gaze to his.

He's emitting that delicious purr again, causing my wolf to stir in my soul. His woodsy scent intrigues me, too. I want to bury my nose against his chest and wrap my arms around his big shoulders, and never let go.

"Is that usually a dress or jeans?" he presses.

I shrug. "A sack." Which I suppose could be like a dress? "I'm okay with this blanket," I tell him. "Thank you."

He stares at me for a long moment before glancing up at Elias. "I'm going to find her something to wear. Can you handle the next group?"

Elias gives him a strange look, one I can't quite define. Amused, maybe? Playful? "Sure," he drawls, his tone holding a funny note to it.

Humor? I think, uncertain. I sometimes heard my brothers use that tone when talking to one another, but I never found the content of their amusement to be very funny.

Enrique brushes his knuckles down my cheek before standing and looking at Elias. "Howl for me if you need me."

"Just send Sven my way," Elias replies. "He can help while you go on your mission." He turns away, then pauses and says, "Don't let Kaz tag along with him. He'll scare the Omegas."

Enrique grunts but doesn't reply, simply walks away and gives me a view of his athletic backside again.

"Are you close to your heat cycle?" Hel asks, the question apparently for me because she's looking right at me.

"I… I don't know. I've never had one." My Alpha put me on suppressants for the last two years, saying something about Alpha Carlos wanting to make my first heat *explosive*. Whatever that meant. "Why do you ask?"

"Because you're eyeing that Alpha like he's a meal you want to devour," she replies, her expression knowing.

"I…" I don't know how to reply to that. Because I can't tell if she's teasing me or chiding me. "He was… kind to me." It sounds lame. But it's all I can think to say in response.

"He was nice," Paige agrees. "They both were."

"That doesn't mean we can trust them," Hel says quietly, her blue gaze scanning our surroundings. "I don't know what's going on, but I'm running the first chance I get."

Guðrún frowns. "They said they'll take us wherever we want to go, so I'm not sure running is wise."

"They'll also catch us," Paige mutters. "X-Clan Alphas are *fast*. Trust me, I know from experience."

"It also sounded like they'll put you in touch with your brother," Guðrún adds. "Are you close to him?"

Hel answers, but I don't quite catch it because Enrique jogs across the field, demonstrating some of that speed Paige just mentioned.

My gaze follows his long, athletic strides, my head tilting to the side.

"You're drooling," Hel drawls loudly.

"Can't really blame her," Paige murmurs, her voice underlined with appreciation. "He's hot. And, as she said, he seems nice."

"*Seems* being the operative word in that sentence," Hel points out.

"They killed Alpha Carlos and all his generals," a new voice informs us as another X-Clan Omega joins our circle. "I wouldn't say they're *nice*, but I definitely consider them an upgrade from the previous regime."

The four of us stare at her, but it's Hel who begins the introductions.

"Wendy" is the new girl's name. Apparently, Elias sent her our way to be part of our group. "I told him I want to go back home, so he said to come sit over here."

My lips curl down at her words. *I don't want to go home.*

But I don't really know where to go.

Will they send me back to my brothers? I wonder, shivering. With my Alpha being dead, I... I don't know if my brothers will even accept me.

They'll probably kill me.

Maybe Hel is right about running...

But where can I even run to?

I have nowhere to go. Nowhere to hide. No one to lean on for support.

I don't even know where I am. Bariloche Sector, obviously. However, I don't know what that's near. I don't even know where any of the sectors the others mentioned are located.

Wildborn Sector.

Savage Sector.

Cusco Sector.

The vampire called her home a *nest*, a term most Omegas would usually consider to be safe. But my nest was never safe. And the vampire herself said there's nowhere for her to go.

My fingers curl into fists, my heart beginning to pound a little too fast. *Calm down,* I tell myself. *You'll upset the Alphas.*

I close my eyes and breathe, the technique one I mastered over the years.

In and out.

In and out.

In... The thought trails off as the scent of evergreens fills my nostrils. *So, so good... Soothing. Addicting.*

I lean toward that scent, only to nearly topple over in the process.

A strong hand catches me before I can fall, his skin hot against my bare shoulder.

"Caja?" Enrique's voice causes my gaze to snap right up to where he's crouching before me.

The other Omegas are silent, their gazes wide.

"Are you all right?" he asks me.

I swallow and nod. "Just, um, maybe hungry?" The term escapes me before I think better of it.

Of course, hearing it aloud reminds me of what Hel said about me looking at Enrique like I want to devour him.

My cheeks heat in response, my thighs tingling with a strange sort of sensation.

Oh, moons, I'm being ridiculous.

I've never acted this way around an Alpha before.

Although, no Alpha has ever been like this one.

Enrique studies me, a little crease forming on his brow. "What do you want to eat?" he asks me.

Hel snorts, then coughs to cover her laugh.

Fortunately, the Alpha ignores her.

I glance at the boxes of food that I haven't touched yet and shrug. "This is fine."

"If it's fine, why haven't you eaten it yet?"

Because I've been distracted, I think, swallowing again. "I'm a little overwhelmed," I say instead.

His expression softens as he sits on the ground next to me. "That's understandable. But you're safe now. All of you," he says, looking at the others. "I realize that's probably hard to believe, and it's going to take some time to trust us. That's fine. We understand."

He holds out something blue for me.

"I wasn't sure of your size, so I found a dress," he explains after I take the fabric from his hands. "Why don't you put that on while I investigate the boxes?"

My fingers run across the texture, my senses suddenly hyperaware of the sensation.

I've never felt anything this soft before. It's so silky and smooth. Everything I wore back home was scratchy or too warm. This feels... *heavenly*.

Dropping the blanket, I work on spreading out the dress to determine the front from the back.

It has sleeves, I marvel. *And it's long*.

So unique.

It's different from what the other Omegas are wearing, too.

Hel has on dark pants and a long-sleeved V-neck shirt with a leather waist cincher. Guðrún is in jeans and a tank top, similar to Paige and Wendy.

And I have this pretty dress, I think, lifting it up to pull over my head. It resembles a waterfall against my skin, sliding downward into place and hugging my svelte form. I go to my knees and do a little shimmy to push it over my hips, then watch it glide over my thighs.

I love it, I decide, placing the blanket beneath me so I don't have to sit on the ground in this beautiful gown. "Thank you," I say, finally looking at Enrique again.

He's staring at me with a look that makes me wonder if he's as starved for food as I am. Because he looks ready to eat me.

The other Omegas have backed away a little, giving us some space. I'm not quite sure why. But I don't mind. Enrique doesn't scare me.

"You're welcome." He clears his throat. "Right, um, food." He rips his gaze away from me and starts shuffling around the boxes.

I don't really pay attention to what he hands me, instead choosing to accept whatever he deigns to give me. However, when he places a water bottle in front of me, I immediately grab it and chug half the contents without bothering to breathe.

It's dangerous.

I have no idea when I'll be gifted with more to drink, but I feel like I haven't had any water in *days*.

Closing my eyes, I savor the hydration and give in to my need to drink more. By the time I finish, the bottle is empty and I nearly whine in protest.

Except two more containers of water have magically appeared before me.

I tentatively reach for one, almost expecting it to be a trick.

When it's not, I accept the small miracle and drink my fill. This time, I have about a fourth left when I'm finally done, and I release a relieved sigh.

Starvation and dehydration are not new concepts for me. Actually, I've learned to live with them. But sometimes being given water is almost worse because I get to a point where I don't feel much at all, then the drink reminds me just how thirsty I really am.

It's a horrible consequence of giving in to my needs.

Fortunately, Enrique hasn't taken the other bottle away.

Actually… I frown down at the blanket around me. *There are three more bottles.* I gape up at him. "Are these all for me?" I ask him.

He shrugs. "I can get more if you need them. But you need to eat, too." He gestures to the items I dropped in favor of the water. I don't even remember doing that. "There's fruit and—"

"Enrique!" Elias calls from the field, his gaze intense as he stares at the other Alpha. "I need your language skills."

Enrique nods. "Be right there," he says in a normal voice, then looks at me once more. "Eat, Caja. I won't be pleased if I come back and find out you haven't touched anything other than water. So please try, okay?"

I shiver, liking his subtle dominance. It's reassuring in a way that pleases my wolf, making me long to obey him. "Yes, Alpha."

"Enrique," he corrects me. "Call me Enrique."

"Yes... Enrique."

He smiles. "Muy bien, pequeño tesoro," he murmurs. *Very good, little treasure.* "I'll be back to check on you in a bit." He runs his knuckles down my cheek like he has a few times before, then pushes away to jog toward Elias.

I enjoy the view again.

Then I focus on the food, just like he requested.

And hope he returns soon.

ENRIQUE

"YOUR BROTHER MADE IT TO ANDORRA SECTOR OKAY," Ander says as he walks toward me. "He's currently sedated and in a padded room."

I nod, a pang of guilt stabbing me in the gut. *I should have gone with him.*

Yet there wasn't anything more I could do for him— or his mate—right now. And being here helping the others clean up my former sector felt better than sitting around, waiting for a doctor to update me on my brother's feral condition.

I'm not even sure if he can be rehabilitated. Being there with him would force me to face that potential fate, which I'm just not ready to embrace. So if I'm being totally honest with myself, I stayed here as a distraction.

And perhaps for a certain little brunette with beautiful eyes, I admit, picturing Caja's pretty face.

37

I checked on her an hour ago and found her sleeping in a makeshift nest made of blankets. The other Omegas in her group were in the nest with her, all of them resting. Exhaustion mingling with relief no doubt knocked them all out.

They likely won't sleep well, but at least they're feeling safe enough to relax for a bit.

I run my fingers through my hair and roll my neck, my muscles cracking along the way. It's been a long few days.

Actually, no. It's been a long few *years*.

Playing Carlos's games for nearly a decade took a toll on my soul. But it was the only way to help my brother. The only way to try to protect his mate and her sister. The only way to beat the bastard at his own schemes.

Carlos was a mastermind, his penchant for chemicals and toxins borderline genius. Unfortunately, he used those talents for nefarious purposes.

To avoid being one of his victims, I pretended to enjoy his pastimes. He rewarded me with a mate, one who chose another over me. Which was fine. I only went along with the mating charade because I knew Carlos would send me Kari as a wedding gift. He thought I favored her among the other Omega playthings. In truth, I just wanted to save her. Because she was the sister of my twin's mate.

Everything I did was with a purpose.

That purpose was finally fulfilled.

So what now? I wonder, glancing around the darkened

field to the few remaining Omega groups left. *Where do I go from here?*

"You all right?" Ander asks, reminding me of his presence. Not that I could forget he stood a few feet away—his Alpha aura basically bled into my skin—but I was a little lost in my thoughts. In the past. The future. *The unknown.*

I clear my throat, debating how to answer him.

I could lie and say I'm fine.

However, I spent the better part of the last ten years pretending to be someone I wasn't. And I am really fucking tired of putting up a false facade.

"Not really," I admit, my palm encircling the back of my neck as I stretch again. "I have no idea how to help Joseph or Savi. I don't think I've ever really known. I just wanted to free them, but now I'm wondering if they'll ever actually be free."

If I should have just let them die, I add to myself, wincing.

It's a horrible thought, one I've been avoiding facing since I found my brother earlier today. Or was it yesterday?

I've lost track of time.

But seeing my brother in that feral state, knowing he couldn't touch his own mate without killing her…

I shake my head. "I knew would be bad. I just…"

"Wasn't prepared for how bad it would actually be," Ander finishes for me. "I get that."

I nod. As the Andorra Sector Alpha, he's probably seen a lot of shit he's never wanted to see. But as the strongest Alpha in his sector, it's his responsibility to handle everything thrown his way and lead by example.

It can't be an easy job. Especially when done the right way. Very unlike Carlos and how he ran Bariloche Sector.

"There's more we need to discuss," Ander tells me. "I know you're dealing with some shit, but this can't wait."

I nod again and fold my arms over my chest. "I understand." Because I know exactly what he wants to discuss—my future.

He said earlier that I was welcome in Andorra Sector to be with my brother.

However, to do that, I have to acknowledge Ander as my superior. It's the only way he can maintain order—if I don't bow to him, I'll be seen as a challenger. And given my age, experience, and former position in Bariloche Sector, I would be considered a worthy opponent.

"Riley says some of the mated Omegas have missing Alphas," he begins, throwing me off completely.

That wasn't at all what I expected him to say, nor was it related to the topic I thought he wanted to address.

"I see," I say slowly, frowning. "What about the Alphas being held near my brother? Have their respective mates been accounted for?" There were a few Betas in the cells as well, but they wouldn't have the same deep-seated connection to an Omega like an Alpha would.

He dips his head in confirmation. "All of those have

been matched by scent. But from what Riley says, we have seven mated Omegas with missing Alphas. Is there anywhere else that he might be keeping them?"

I frown, considering the question. "Carlos liked keeping everything and everyone close to his personal compound. He had trust issues." Hence all the Alphas and Betas he locked up in cages, and the wicked torture he inflicted on those with mate bonds.

Ander releases a low growl, his agitation palpable. "Riley seems pretty certain the Alphas are alive. Otherwise, the Omegas in question wouldn't be coherent at all."

True. They would be catatonic and unresponsive, something Carlos would have wanted to avoid for his little *toys*.

I rack my brain, trying to think of where he may have imprisoned other Alphas, but I meant what I said —Carlos had trust issues. I was commonly considered to be one of Carlos's highest-ranking generals, yet I only had access to his Omega operation. And that access came with a myriad of restrictions.

Fortunately, my position afforded me a wealth of intimate knowledge regarding his procedures and the ins and outs of his compound—a fact that had made me a valuable asset in our infiltration of Bariloche Sector this week.

However, that knowledge didn't extend to all of Carlos's dungeons or how he controlled the Alphas who protested his rule. I was familiar with his penchant for psychedelics, but not the full scope of his prison system.

"I'm only aware of the dungeon he kept under his

compound." And I really only knew about that because of my twin. I'd felt his presence there for years, despite Carlos claiming he was dead. "He wasn't the type to house anything of value too far from his estate, though. So I can't imagine there are more dungeons hidden in Bariloche Sector."

And if there were any, they're now destroyed, thanks to Kazek and Sven blowing up every structure in Bariloche earlier today. They wanted to ensure the entire sector would be uninhabitable. Any surviving Alphas are officially rogues. A few sectors might accept them into their territories; most will not.

The Betas are another situation entirely, mostly because they never had a choice in how Carlos ran his sector. A whole line of Betas are currently waiting to be interviewed for potential entry into Andorra, Norse, or Winter.

Meanwhile, the Omegas will be taken anywhere they choose, assuming they're coherent and well enough to make a choice. Those who weren't able are already in Andorra for medical treatment, the last flight having left hours ago to take them to safety.

The only Omegas left are the ones who are in a healthy enough condition to voice their desires.

"Do you think he would have traded any of the Alphas to other sectors?" Ander asks, his expression hardening.

I shake my head. "They wouldn't have been much use to them. I mean, you saw the state my brother's in…" I trail off and clear my throat. "But if the Alpha in question offended a friend, perhaps Carlos would trade the Alpha away as recompense. However, seven is a high number." And Carlos wasn't one to give up his resources.

Unless he was tired of caring for those resources.

In which case...

"It's possible he has them rotting somewhere," I say, thinking aloud. "Somewhere he can't smell them or hear them. Somewhere they can't escape. But I have no idea where that would be. Maybe one of his many trading points. Or, more likely, in a place no one would ever think to visit."

"That's not helpful," Ander mutters.

"I know. But that's how Carlos worked—he never made anything easy." Hence the intricate assault on Bariloche Sector. Carlos left traps everywhere, turning his lands into a literal minefield, one we navigated all the way to his compound.

Ander blows out a frustrated breath. "Well, maybe Riley can find out more from the Omegas, then." He grimaces. "Assuming any of them can be woken up."

"Some of the other Alphas may know, too," I say. "Knowing Carlos, he tortured them with potential fates. Perhaps one of his former taunts will reveal where the missing Alphas are being kept."

Ander nods. "All right." He crosses his arms, his stance rivaling mine. "So tell me about this Omega you're interested in."

I arch a brow. "Who says I'm interested in an Omega?"

"Elias. And he's an excellent judge of character. But we've started a new program in Andorra Sector that

43

requires our Alphas to woo the Omegas, not just claim them. I hope that won't be a problem for you."

He says that last part like it's a threat more than an explanation, making it clear that if I do have a problem with this, then *we* are going to have a problem.

"Winter and Kari can vouch for my opinions on consent and *wooing*," I inform him flatly. Although, I can't help the twinge of sarcasm on the final word, because who says *wooing*? Ander Cain, apparently.

"Hmm," he hums. "You're alive, so you must have treated both Omegas well. Otherwise, Kaz and my brother would have killed you by now." There's a hint of amusement underlining his tone, but I have a hard time believing he's truly amused.

Something tells me Ander rarely finds humor in much of anything.

"Has she said where she wants to go yet?" he goes on, slightly changing topics. "Your Omega, I mean."

"She's not my Omega," I correct him. "And no, I don't believe she has."

"That's not what Elias said," he drawls.

I frown. "She told him where she wants to go?"

"I was referring to the *not my Omega* bullshit you just spewed," he tells me, his expression now matching his amused tone.

Maybe I was wrong. Maybe Ander Cain can find humor in things.

"He said you practically shoved him out of the way when he tried to talk to her," Ander goes on. "He was surprised you didn't piss all over her, too."

I roll my eyes. "Your Second exaggerates."

"He does," Ander agrees. "But as I said, he's an excellent judge of character."

I grunt. "We just met."

"In my experience, that matters little to our wolves."

Well, he's right about that. My wolf sniffed Caja out in that cage, her scent immediately intriguing him. Then those pretty eyes found mine, and my world went sideways.

"You're a good Alpha, Enrique," Ander continues. "I'll respect whatever decision you make regarding the Omega. Just make sure she agrees with said decision. It'll make your life a lot easier."

"That sounds like another statement driven by experience," I tell him, ignoring his comment about me being a *good Alpha*. I'm not even sure what that means anymore.

"You have no fucking idea," he mutters as a message populates the air over his wrist. "Dušan," he says to me. "Shadowland Sector Alpha. I need to take this."

He doesn't wait for me to reply, just steps away to pick up the call.

I leave to give him privacy. Sector politics isn't my thing. I'll refer that to the Alpha in charge.

And in the interim, I'll go check on Caja.

My Omega, I think, liking the way that sounds. I've been around Omegas all my life, but I've never considered any of them in this manner, likely because Carlos's rules made it impossible to want to claim a female for my own.

Perhaps that adds to my intrigue.

Or maybe it's just Caja.

45

Regardless, I wander over to where she's sleeping and crouch down to pull her blanket back up to her chin. She leans into my touch, her lips parting on a sigh.

"Rest, pequeño tesoro," I whisper as I resist the urge to stroke her cheek. "You're safe now. I won't let anyone hurt you again. I promise."

CAJA

Growling stirs me from my slumber, the sound loud and fierce to my ears. I curl deeper into my nest, trying to escape what happens next.

The screams, I think, shuddering. *So. Many. Screams.*

I try to drown it out, to pretend I'm somewhere else. But there's nowhere for me to imagine. All I've ever known is hell.

Wake up.

Obey.

Survive.

Try to sleep.

That's my life. My solitary existence. Until my Alpha takes me to my fate.

Please, I pray to the moons. *Please don't make it as bad as I fear.*

But I've heard the terror in the others' cries. I know it's even worse than I can imagine.

If only I could dream of somewhere safe, if just for a moment.

Murmurs fall around me, that growling sound reaching a crescendo.

I hold my breath and wait, my mind searching for an escape.

Dark eyes. Even darker hair. A perfect nose. Square jaw dusted in fine black stubble. A smile with dimples.

I frown, the picture so vivid inside my mind that I could swear I've seen this male before. But... but where?

Why...? My eyes fly open as the man's name graces my thoughts. *Enrique.*

I glance around, startled to find a brightly illuminated field.

My focus shifts to the air where a jet soars toward the midday sun. That was the source of rumbling that woke me. I've seen planes before, as my Alpha lived near an old airport. All the overseas shipments went through there, many of them carrying terrified passengers.

Their screams...

I swallow.

Those screams will haunt me until I die.

But there are no screams here, just murmurs.

I follow the source of said murmurs and find several Omegas huddled nearby. *Hel. Paige. Wendy. Guðrún.* The other two are new. Neither of them is an X-Clan Omega either.

"That's from your Alpha," Hel says, gesturing with her chin toward a pack near my nest of blankets.

"M-my Alpha?" I repeat, a shiver traversing my spine. *My Alpha is here?*

"Enrique," Guðrún murmurs.

It's a single word. A name. And yet the profound

relief that rolls through my shoulders nearly has me melting into my blankets.

Not Bautista. *Enrique.*

Because my Alpha is dead.

And I'm safe. Sort of, anyway. I... I have no home. But my Alpha isn't here. He's gone. *Forever.*

"He brought all of us lunch," Paige adds with a dreamy smile. "But he put yours in that sack to keep it warm and asked us not to wake you."

"Oh." I pluck at the pack and peek inside.

My eyes widen at finding a banana, a sandwich, two bottles of water, and what looks like a cookie.

"Apparently, one of the jets arrived with more food," Paige says before I can ask where all this came from. "Then they turned around and left with another group of Omegas."

"Yeah, there are only three groups left," Hel adds. "Elias says everyone will be leaving by nightfall, so we need to tell him where we want to go. He almost woke you to ask for your choice, but your Alpha stopped him."

My nose crinkles. "My Alpha being Enrique?" I ask, making sure that's who she means.

"Yes. The meal you're craving."

I blink at her. She has a strange obsession with referring to Enrique as food. Still, ignoring that, I reply, "I don't know where I want to go."

"Then they'll take you to Andorra Sector by default," Paige tells me. "That's what they told Guðrún."

The Vampire Omega shrugs. "It'll give me some

49

time to think."

I'm not sure what she means by that, and the haunted look in her gaze makes me not want to ask. So I just nod like I understand and rummage through the pack from Enrique.

I'm halfway through my sandwich when the male in question approaches with another Alpha at his side. "Good morning, Caja," Enrique purrs.

Well, he doesn't literally purr. But in my head, I swear I hear his gentle hum.

Actually, I think I heard him purring all night. Perhaps in my dreams?

"This is Sven," he continues. "He's from Norse Sector."

"Hi, Caja," the blond Alpha murmurs, crouching. "Enrique asked me to tell you about my homeland."

I frown. "Why?"

"In case you want to come live in my sector," he says.

I glance at Enrique. "Is that where you live?" I'm actually not sure where he's from. But maybe I can go wherever he is, assuming other Alphas are like him.

Enrique winces. "No, I'm from Bariloche Sector."

My lips form an "O" shape, yet the sound doesn't leave my mouth. I… I'm not sure how to respond. I thought maybe he was from a land of kind Alphas. Apparently not.

And I don't think staying here with him is an option.

Unless they take me back to my brothers, I think, grimacing.

"But you're planning to go back to Andorra Sector

for a while, right?" Sven says, his comment clearly for Enrique.

He runs his fingers through his thick hair, something I've seen him do a few times now. The strands tickle his ears, suggesting that maybe it's a bit longer than he's used to. But I like the length. It gives him a somewhat wild appeal. "Yeah, that's the plan. For now."

Sven nods. "It's a good plan."

Enrique gives him a look. "I'm sure your brother feels similarly." His sarcasm is evident in his tone, but it just makes the other man chuckle.

"He's used to managing intimidating Alphas and fending off challengers."

"I won't challenge your brother," Enrique tells him.

"Oh, I know. But I don't think you'll submit to him either."

Enrique shrugs. "I might." But then his gaze returns to me. "Sven will tell you more about Norse Sector, in case that's where you would like to go."

"What if I want to go with you?" I ask before I can think better of my bold question. "I… I mean…" *Crap. Why did I say that?*

However, he doesn't seem to mind my boldness. Because he smiles in response. "You're welcome to go with me, pequeño tesoro. In fact, I would very much like that. But Sven had to offer an alternative."

"Just following Ander's new courtship rules," Sven drawls. "I'll let him know her choice."

He leaves before I can tell him I haven't actually made a choice. Not one I vocalized, anyway.

But I… I like the idea of following Enrique.

Besides, several of the other Omegas are going there, too. And they've been pretty nice to me so far. Mostly, that is.

Hel likes to tease me, but not in the same way the Omegas teased me back home. She smiles and shares information. The Omegas in my Alpha's nest never smiled, and they certainly never *shared* anything either. No food. No water. No kind words. Just... barbs and cruelties.

Enrique brushes his knuckles down my cheek, an action he's done several times now. I like it. It's almost like a mark, his scent embedding itself into my skin. I lean into his touch and inhale, his woodsy cologne surrounding me.

"The jets will be leaving around sunset," he tells me before glancing at the others. "There are showers on board that you all can use once you're in the air. New clothes will also be available, but sizes will vary."

"Will you be on the jet?" I ask, embracing my bold streak and hoping he still likes it.

His answering grin tells me he does, but it's a short-lived expression as he replies, "I don't know yet. But once I have my assignment, I'll share it with you."

Something about that feels like a promise. An intimate vow. It has my wolf wagging excitedly in me, like she's pleased this Alpha is favoring us.

Is he? I wonder, staring into his dark eyes. *Does he feel as drawn to me as I am to him?*

I don't get a chance to ask because someone calls his name from the field, pulling him away from our group.

He sends me a wink before he leaves, the look one I commit to memory.

"You should be careful," one of the unnamed X-Clan Omegas cautions. "I was talking to a Beta earlier, and he warned me that Enrique was one of Carlos's favored generals. He's not a good Alpha."

My brow furrows, her description at odds with my instincts.

"It's true," the other unnamed Omega says. "I heard their conversation. He was saying how he didn't understand why the Alphas have let Enrique live after everything he's done."

The original Omega nods. "Yes, exactly."

"Maybe he helped the other Alphas stop whatever was happening here," Guðrún offers, her voice soft. "They all seem to be friends."

They do, I think, agreeing with her. *If Enrique's bad, the others wouldn't be so friendly with him.*

But knowing he's from here does make me a little uneasy. *Did he know my Alpha?* I wonder.

Of course he did, I realize in the next instant. *Enrique knew my Alpha's name, and he told me he was dead.*

He didn't seem all that upset about the loss, though. So maybe they weren't friends, just acquaintances.

"Well, I don't trust him," the first X-Clan Omega says with a flip of her long brown hair.

"Same," the other agrees.

Guðrún shrugs. "His intentions feel safe to me." Her nose crinkles after she says it, like she's surprised by her own words. But then she glances at me and adds, "He seems very fond of you."

53

Hel snorts. "Because she's about to go into heat."

I blink. "What?"

"You can't feel it?" she asks me.

"She said she's never gone into heat before," Paige interjects. "So she wouldn't know what it feels like. Not only that, but our estrous cycles are individualized, which means we all go into heat at our own pace."

Wendy nods. "Yes, that. I assume that's why the Alphas are trying to get us all to a sector sooner rather than later. Odds are high that at least one of us will be going into heat soon, and they want to protect us."

"Or breed you," one of the unnamed Omegas mutters. "That's why I want to go home."

"Same," the other echoes.

Paige's gaze narrows. "Well, I have no interest in returning to Cusco Sector."

The other two females scoff and huddle together. I don't know if they knew each other before coming here or if they met in their group. Regardless, they seem to be bonded by similarity.

Ignoring them, I think about what Hel said regarding my heat.

I don't feel any different.

Well, that's not true.

I feel satisfied. Full. *Hydrated.* That was certainly different from my norm.

"What sort of changes…" I trail off as movement to my right catches my gaze.

Elias and another Alpha are walking toward us; Enrique is nowhere in sight.

Goose bumps pebble down my arms, the Alpha with

Elias exuding a dominant air that makes it impossible to meet his gaze. He's powerful. In charge. And commands attention.

"All right," he says, his voice gruff. "We've been able to make arrangements for most of you to go where you've requested." He pulls out a clipboard and starts reading. "Hel, Alpha Ragnar is expecting you in Savage Sector."

Hel perks up at that, her blue gaze bright. "You spoke to my brother?"

The Alpha glances up. "No. Alpha Dušan was able to pull some strings. Savage Sector isn't all that accessible, but we've found a way to make this work for you."

She nods.

He continues by addressing the two unnamed Omegas—*Farah* and *Latya*, I learn—and tells them he's not been successful in contacting their Alpha. "You're going to Norse Sector for now. Alpha Alana is going to take over trying to reach your home sector."

The two females share a look, uncertainty written on their faces.

But the Alpha doesn't give them room to debate or make further requests. He simply tells them they need to go join a group across the field.

"You're on the next flight out," he informs them before moving on to me, Guðrún, and Paige. "I don't have room on my jet to fly you directly Andorra Sector with us, so Enrique is going to bring you there after he's done dropping off everyone else."

Wendy is the last one he addresses, confirming she'll be taken back to Tallinn Sector.

"There are four other Omegas joining you all on the journey, bringing the total count up to nine. Everything is prearranged, but you will be traveling for a few days. Should you need anything, Enrique is your Alpha. He'll do whatever he can to make you comfortable. Understood?"

Those of us who are left—Farah and Latya already ran off to the other group—nod.

"Good." He looks at me, Paige, and Guðrún again. "In case you're unaware, I'm Ander Cain, the Alpha of Andorra Sector."

"You probably should have started the conversation that way," Elias drawls.

Ander ignores him and adds, "We're very pleased with your choice to join us. Accommodations are already being prepared for you, and we look forward to welcoming you into your new homes, however temporary they may be."

He gives a little bow of his head and turns away without saying anything else.

"Not bad, Cain," Elias says as he trails after him. "Kat would approve."

"Stop goading me, E," Ander replies.

Elias presses a palm to his chest. "Would I do such a thing?"

"Every fucking day of my life," the Alpha of Andorra Sector growls.

Elias chuckles, their conversation quieting as they make quick work of the field with their long strides.

"Well, he's terrifying," Paige whispers.

"Yeah," Hel agrees. "He reminds me a bit of my brother."

I say nothing, my gaze searching for Enrique as I recall what Ander said. *"Should you need anything, Enrique is your Alpha."*

Enrique is going to be our escort to Andorra Sector.

He's our Alpha.

My Alpha.

Farah and Latya's warnings play through my mind, eliciting a shiver down my spine.

Can I trust him? I wonder. *I want to trust him.*

Because the notion of him being my Alpha is quite appealing. Perhaps a little *too* appealing.

Maybe I am about to go into heat.

I just hope it doesn't happen on the plane...

ENRIQUE

"You good?" Elias asks as I do a final check in the cockpit.

I nod. "Yeah, like riding a bike." Only easier, honestly. Andorra Sector's technology is leagues ahead of the rest of the world.

Well, *most* of the world.

The V-Clan wolves have their own fancy shit empowered by their voodoo magic. But in terms of X-Clan tech, Andorra Sector is top-notch.

"All right." Elias claps me on the shoulder. "Don't knot the Omega on the jet. You have no copilot, and while the autopilot system is good, it's not *that* good."

I arch a brow at him. "I know how to control my wolf, Elias."

He grins. "Yeah, but he's chomping at the bit to sink his teeth into that Omega. I can see it in your eyes every time you look at her."

"We just met."

"As I said yesterday, that means shit."

"I think you told me it meant little to our wolves," I correct him.

"Same thing," he tells me before turning to leave. Then he pauses and adds, "Thanks for doing this."

"It's the least I can do after everything you all have done for me," I reply, meaning it.

When Ander said he needed someone to take a group of Omegas to their sectors of choice, I volunteered for the job. It seemed like an appropriate task for me.

And it also prolonged the inevitable reunion with my brother.

"We didn't do it for you," he murmurs.

"I know." They did it for Kari. "But I benefited." Because Carlos is finally fucking dead. My brother is free... to an extent. Kari and Savi are safe.

And I'm... in a to-be-determined state.

"I think that remains to be seen," he says, his expression knowing. He can't read my mind, but he no doubt understands my current predicament. "See you in a day or two. Then we'll talk more."

He claps me on the shoulder again and exits. I finalize a few items while the Omegas board, Elias's voice traveling to my ears as he instructs them all on where to sit.

"You'll be welcome to move around after takeoff," he's saying, providing an overview of takeoff procedures.

The Omegas don't say much, but their nervous

energy speaks volumes. For some of them, this is probably their first time on a jet. And the others who have flown before—to reach Bariloche Sector—likely didn't enjoy their previous flight experiences.

"All right, Captain. You're all set and cleared for takeoff."

I glance back at Elias, my eyebrow cocked. "Your imitation game needs some work." Because he just attempted—and miserably failed—to do a radio controller's scratchy tone, like he was mimicking some old movie from the Pre-Infected Era.

He chuckles. "You and I are going to have some fun when you get to Andorra Sector."

"Why does that sound like a threat?"

Amusement flashes in his midnight gaze. "Because I'm the best shot in all of Andorra Sector, and I just picked you as a new sparring partner, amigo."

I smirk. "You should have vetted me before challenging me, *amigo*."

"I vetted you yesterday when we took down Carlos. You didn't miss a single target." He cants his head. "As I said, we're going to have some fun together." He steps out of the cockpit. "Fly safe."

"You, too," I tell him.

He nods and closes the cockpit door. It locks automatically, not that it's really needed. But the jet is equipped with safety features, just in case.

Less than a minute later, a green light appears as the outer door is secured, telling me he has officially disembarked the jet. I pull on my headset and do a final check, then focus on the cameras to find a Beta waving a flag.

There isn't a runway, but these high-tech jets shoot upward like a rocket. Very, very different from the planes of my youth when humans still ran the world.

"All clear," Sven says, acting as my land crew. "Enjoy the skies."

"Always," I reply.

My animal prefers the ground, while I prefer the sky. I was probably meant to be born as a dragon shifter or something else with wings. Alas, I'm a wolf.

My beast growls inside, like he can understand my thoughts. Or perhaps it's the knowledge of what I'm about to do that has him agitated.

Flipping a switch on my headset, I initiate the speaker system within the jet. "We're about to take off," I warn them all. "We'll be heading straight upward, so please make sure you're seated and your seatbelts are fastened."

Elias already went through that spiel, buckling them all in before he deboarded, but I check the video feed just to be certain and find nine nervous Omegas strapped into the passenger bay.

"Once we're in the air, you'll be free to move about the cabin. The room at the back has a closet of clothes, and the bathroom was stocked to meet your needs as well. I suggest you take turns, as it's not a large space." I checked it before going into the cockpit. The shower is big enough for two or three Omegas, but I doubt it'll be comfortable.

I scan the security feed, searching for any signs of distress. Apart from a few anxious glances, they all seem to be okay.

"All right, taking off in ten seconds…" I toggle another switch to initiate the system's takeoff protocols.

An artificial feminine voice continues the countdown overhead.

"Nine."

"Eight."

"Seven."

I shift my gaze away from the Omegas on the screen and focus on the controls before me. Most of this is automated, but I still have to monitor the process.

"Six."

"Five."

I check my belt.

"Four."

I fix my gaze on the window as a subtle rumble begins beneath me, causing adrenaline to pump through my veins.

"Three."

"Two."

"One."

The rumble grows into a roar as the jet shoots upward into the sky, the g-forces pressing on every inch of my body as we ascend at an incredible speed. It's an initial reaction to the rapid acceleration, but as the artificial gravity inside the cabin equalizes, the crushing sensation slowly lessens.

Only to heighten once more as the jet begins to arc, pushing us into our desired flight path.

I programmed it before takeoff, but I check the direction to be sure we're heading the correct way, and we are. We'll fly north, hugging the coastline until we reach the northernmost point of this continent and begin a path to the east.

Everything begins to settle as the jet reaches its cruising speed, the heaviness leaving my form and gradually returning me to normal. Or almost normal, anyway.

Glancing at the screen, I see several of the Omegas shaking out their arms and legs, likely having not enjoyed the experience. But no one appears to be getting sick, so that's a good sign.

I give it a few more minutes before I click over to the speaker system again. "We've reached our cruising altitude. I'm not sure if Ander or Elias shared our complete itinerary, but we'll be heading up to Nova Sector first, where we'll be spending the night and restocking."

I've never been to Nova Sector before. It's one of the few remaining areas in the world harboring Arctic wolves, as their kind is unfortunately susceptible to the zombielike virus that wiped out most of the human population.

When Ander called to tell them he had two Arctic Omegas in his possession, the Alpha of Nova Sector had been a mixture of furious and relieved. Apparently, the two white-haired females were the only unmated Omegas in his sector.

They were also his daughters.

Thus, Ander suggested that Nova Sector be our first stop.

From a flight path point of view, it made the most sense. After Nova Sector, we'll head over to Savage Sector in what used to be Romania. Then Tallinn Sector, and two other places in Asia, before eventually making our way to Andorra Sector.

I return my attention to the security feed, my gaze instantly finding Caja.

She's coming back with me.

Paige, too.

However, it's Caja that holds my attention.

She's sitting quietly, listening to Hel as she asks the two Arctic wolves about Nova Sector. The Ulv wolf sounds nervous, which is interesting because she's come off as one of the more confident Omegas. Although, right now, she almost looks ill.

Probably from takeoff, I think, noting a few other pale Omegas on the security feed.

Caja seems okay, though. Just concerned. However, as the Arctic wolves continue describing their home, she and a few of the others start to relax.

I follow suit, leaning back in my chair and checking the controls again.

We'll be in the air for several hours. While these jets move quickly, they can't exactly teleport. Alas, we'll be here for a bit. More than long enough for all the Omegas to shower, change, rest, and eat.

I roll my neck, my muscles tight from what feels like years of stress. And it's not going away anytime soon.

Sighing, I stare out the window.

It's a clear night, the nearly full moon illuminating the dark sky. Perfect flying weather.

Checking the radar, I don't see any storms in our path. And none on the horizon.

Should be a fairly straightforward flight.

I unbuckle my harness and stand to stretch my arms. I haven't slept in days, not that I really need it. But I can't fight the urge to yawn. Because fuck, I'm tired. *So. Fucking. Tired.*

And there's no end in sight, I think darkly, my shoulders falling.

When I agreed to pilot this flight, I didn't consider the potential downtime.

"Fuck," I mutter, leaning against a wall. The last thing I want is to be left alone with my thoughts. My regrets. My worries. My *everything*.

Closing my eyes, I steal a deep breath, then go back to stare at the monitor, hoping to find my little treasure. My *distraction*. But she's no longer seated in her chair from takeoff.

I flick through the feeds, searching for her. And pause when I find her.

She's… she's standing outside the cockpit door.

I turn toward it, surprised by her presence.

Yet she hasn't made a sound.

Frowning, I look back at the monitor to see her chewing on her lower lip, her gaze uncertain. She takes a step back, then pauses, her expression turning determined.

Only for her to lose the determination as her hand rises.

65

My lips twitch as she curls her fingers into fists, clearly agitated with herself.

I may not be able to read her mind, but I can read her expression clear as day. She's debating whether or not to knock, and she's frustrated with herself for not just doing it.

I could help her and just open the door. However, I kind of want to see how this plays out. So I lean against the wall instead, my gaze on the camera as she continues to battle with herself.

It's cute. One second, she's nodding. The next, she's wincing.

I swear I hear her growling through the door as she spins around to storm off toward the main cabin. I'm about to go after her when she turns right back toward the cockpit and practically runs toward me.

Her knock is abrupt. One quick pound, then she jumps back with a look of horror in her expression like she can't believe she just did that.

I chuckle in response, more amused than I think I have been in a long time.

But as I unlock and open the door, I don't let her see my humored reaction. I simply peek my head out and utter a polite "Everything all right, tesoro?"

She blinks big dark eyes at me. "I, uh, was wondering if you need anything to eat?"

I push the door a little wider so I can lean against the frame. "That depends," I say, looking her up and down. "What's on the menu?" I've been a little soft with her until now, not really flirting with her so much as comforting her. However, that little show I just witnessed put me in a playful mood. And now I want to see how she'll respond to some clear flirtation.

Alas, she just blinks at me and starts reciting actual food items.

So innocent, I marvel, looking over her again. *And so damn beautiful.*

She swallows. "Does any of that sound, um, good?"

"None of those items suit my current mood." Because it's not food I'm in the mood for. But I don't tell her that last part.

"Oh." Her nose scrunches. "Okay. Well, if you change your mind, let me know and I'll bring you something."

"Thank you," I say to her, smiling. "It was thoughtful of you to check on me."

She nods. "You're welcome. I'll just be…" She gestures back to the main cabin and takes a step away from me.

"I wouldn't mind some company, though," I tell her before she can escape me. "It's kind of lonely in here." A lame comment, but a truthful one.

Her eyes flash up to mine. "Oh. Is it okay for me to be up here?"

I shrug. "I'm the pilot, so I suppose that means I make the rules, and I say it's fine."

"You're also an Alpha," she points out. "So I think you always make the rules."

I consider that and nod. "True, dominance is a natural trait. But I've never really been in a position where my rules mattered." Because I was always carrying out Carlos's wishes—or, most recently, Ander's wishes—but never my own.

Caja frowns at me. "I thought you were one of Alpha Carlos's generals. Wouldn't that have put you in a position to create and enforce rules?"

My heart squeezes at her words. "You know I used to be one of his generals?" Did someone tell her that? Or did she recognize my name after I shared it?

No. It couldn't be the latter. She would have feared me if that were the case.

But then, why doesn't she fear me now?

"W-well, no," she stammers, her tan skin paling.

Never mind. There's the fear.

Shit.

"Another Omega told me," she goes on. "I wasn't sure if it was true or not."

I grab the back of my neck and blow out a breath. "Yes, I was one of his generals. One of his favorites, actually." I didn't really need to add that last part, but I want her to know me. To *understand* me.

"I… I shouldn't have asked," she says, taking a step back. "I know it's not my place. I…" She frowns. "I don't know why I'm acting this way around you. I'm sorry, Alpha."

"It's Enrique," I remind her gently. "And what way do you mean? How are you acting around me?"

She glances over her shoulder before leaning toward me and whispering, "I keep asking you questions. I know I'm not supposed to. I… I've never done this before."

"You've never asked questions?"

She shakes her head, her eyes widening. "Never. My Alpha would have killed me for behaving this way."

"Your Alpha," I echo. "As in your father, Bautista?"

Caja visibly shivers, then dips her chin. "Yes. I wasn't allowed to speak to him."

I stare down at her. "You couldn't speak to him?"

She shakes her head again. "I wasn't worthy of his presence."

"He told you that?" I ask, my blood heating at the notion. *Your father called you unworthy, and all I did was shoot him in the head?*

Fuck.

Had I known any of this, I would have taken out his knees first. Let him suffer for a few hours. *Then* put a bullet between his eyes.

Her brow furrows. "Yes, as did all the others."

The others? Multiple people called her worthless? "Who are the others?" I ask aloud, prepared to take mental notes. Because whoever they are, I'm going to fucking annihilate them.

"My pack," she tells me. "The other Alphas—my brothers, I guess. And the Omegas. They all explained my uselessness, so I understand. My only worth in life is whatever price Alpha Carlos agreed to pay for me, which I gathered wasn't much."

I suddenly want to punch something. Or someone. Several someones.

It takes physical effort not to outwardly react to her words. But I don't want to scare her with my anger.

"Carlos was a monster, Caja," I reply, my voice a bit more gravelly than usual. "He couldn't define your worth, even if he tried. Because he never appreciated the beauty and rarity of Omega kind. He only ever sought to profit off the exploitation of those we—Alphas —are meant to care for and cherish."

She blinks at me. "But… but you worked for him."

"I did. And I helped kill him."

"Why?"

"Because I hated him." It's a simple response, one I have no trouble uttering.

"Why?" she repeats, her eyes inquisitive.

"It's a very long story," I admit.

She winces, her gaze lowering to my chest. "I'm sorry, Alpha. I shouldn't have asked. It's not my place to request explanations."

I reach forward to take her chin between my fingers and guide her eyes back to mine. "Please call me Enrique, Caja. There's no need to be formal with me."

She swallows. "I'm sorry."

"No more apologies either," I tell her, my thumb stroking her jaw. "You're more than welcome to talk to me, pequeño tesoro. In fact, I encourage it."

Her brow is still furrowed, her expression uncertain.

"I wasn't saying it's a long story to deter you, Caja. I was going to ask again if you would like to come into the cockpit, as I would much prefer to sit down before I tell you all about my history with Carlos."

"You really don't mind?"

"I really don't," I tell her softly. "Actually, it's the opposite; I would love for you to join me." I release her to gesture to the chairs behind me. "There are even two seats. And the view up here is pretty awesome."

She glances around me to see the large glass windows. Her eyes round at the sight. "Wow."

"I know," I murmur. "So what do you say, Caja? Want to keep me company while I fly the plane?"

Her bottom lip disappears between her teeth as she considers me once more. Then, ever so gradually, she nods. "Yes, please."

I smile and step to the side. "Then come on in and make yourself comfortable."

CAJA

I listen as Enrique tells me all about his twin brother, Joseph. And his brother's mate, Savi. Then about her sister, Kari.

About all the things Carlos did to them.

How he tortured Joseph and Savi for mating one another.

How Carlos tormented any Alpha for claiming an Omega.

But he was particularly cruel to Joseph because Savi was Carlos's daughter.

"He didn't take kindly to Joseph claiming her," Enrique says. "But it was irreversible once done. So Kari, Carlos's other daughter, took the brunt of his anger and frustration."

Enrique describes what some of that means without going into too much detail. But it's enough.

The whole situation is complicated and heartbreaking.

He continues by telling me about having to agree to marry a Beta to help firm up an alliance with another sector. "Carlos offered it like it was a gift for being so loyal to him, but I knew better. It was a command," he says.

But then he explains how the marriage never went through.

She ended up being an Omega who mated another Alpha. "She snuck onto his plane during our betrothal dinner," Enrique muses. "That Alpha was Kazek, whom I don't think you met, but he was part of the raid this week."

I nod, enthralled by this entire story.

It gets even more interesting as he tells me that Kari was also on that plane because Kazek's friend kidnapped her from the party. Or rather, *saved* her.

"I ended up going to Norse Sector to meet with them under the guise of looking for my former betrothed, but really, I just wanted to find Kari." His lips twist into a smile. "Turns out, she didn't need rescuing. The Alpha who took her from the party—Sven—did that for me."

"How?"

"That's their story to tell, but they're mated now. And she seems happy." He clears his throat. "But to help condense a very long tale, Sven wanted to take down Carlos as a way to avenge Kari. I offered to help. We succeeded, and here we are."

Wow. I'm not only stunned by his story but also by the fact that he just shared all these details with me. "Were you upset about your betrothed mating another

Alpha?" I wonder aloud, somewhat caught up on that point of his history.

He was engaged to another woman. An Omega *in disguise.*

My wolf growls inside me, clearly agitated by this discovery. Or maybe she can just sense my own discomfort with this knowledge.

"No," Enrique murmurs. "I was never interested in the marriage. I only went along with it because I suspected Carlos would give me Kari as a wedding gift. I wanted to save her."

So this is all about Kari, then. "Do you love her?" It's an intrusive question, yet I... I can't help but ask it. *Is he heartbroken that another Alpha saved her and claimed her?* My stomach twists with the notion, my heart skipping a few beats.

"As a sister, yes," he replies. "I used to visit her in the dungeons. It served two purposes—it convinced Carlos I was the monster he intended for me to be and allowed me to check up on her. He had no idea all I ever did for her was purr."

My insides churn again at the mention of him purring for another female. Another *Omega*. I want his purr to be for me and only for me. Which isn't fair. This Alpha isn't mine, even if he is kind to me.

"You do have a very nice purr," I tell him, my cheeks warming with the admission.

He smiles. "Yeah?" He brushes his knuckles against my cheek, the action one I'm starting to love more than anything else in this world. "Thank you, pequeño tesoro. I can purr for you whenever you'd like."

Now would be amazing, I think, but I don't have the

courage to utter the words. So I just nod, my face burning even hotter, especially where he just touched me.

"Anyway, that's a very long explanation of why I hate Carlos and how I helped kill him." He leans back in his chair, his large body angled toward mine. "I've done a lot of things I'm not proud of, Caja. Being Carlos's general was about survival, but it doesn't excuse everything I've done, everything I've had to do."

A haunting gleam enters his black eyes, giving them an ominous glow.

I swallow, somewhat uncomfortable with that glimmer. Primarily because I often see it reflected in the mirror when looking at myself.

"I'll understand if you don't want to be around me," he continues. "Especially if I remind you of Bautista. He might not have been one of Carlos's generals like I was, but he managed a piece of the operation, making us similar in that regard."

I frown. "You're nothing like my former Alpha." He would never have talked to me like this, let alone even looked at me.

Enrique makes me feel… *seen*. He makes me feel important. He makes me feel *safe*.

"You're nothing like him," I repeat, staring into his dark eyes. "You're…" *Mine*, a soft voice whispers inside me, my wolf humming in agreement.

His gaze holds mine, his expression seeming to darken. But not in a frightening way. His eyes… his eyes are… *intense*. His lips are full. His cheekbones look like they're cut from marble. His face is just so incredibly handsome. So masculine, yet beautiful. I want to trace his jaw with my finger. Lick the dimple on his cheek. Nibble his plump bottom lip.

"Caja," he whispers.

"Alpha," I return, my body tingling all over. It feels like my veins are on fire and the only way to cool down is to touch this man. This Alpha. This impressive wolf.

I reach for him, suddenly emboldened with the need to stroke him. To caress the stubble on his jaw. To crawl into his lap and *kiss* him.

His mouth parts, the movement seeming like an invitation.

I push off of my chair, ready to accept, only to fall back into it as a crashing sound echoes throughout the cabin. Enrique instantly straightens, his gaze flying to the windows. "What the hell?" he says, a series of alarms suddenly sounding all around us. "It was fucking clear!"

I don't know what he means, and I don't have a chance to ask because a bolt of lightning has me flinching backward against my seat.

"Fuck!" he shouts, his hands flying around the cockpit as he starts dealing with the alarms. Or I assume that's what he's doing, anyway. He grabs a headset and pulls it over his head. "Everyone find a seat and buckle up!" The command in his voice is all Alpha, causing my wolf to whimper inside.

I flounder in my chair, trying to figure out how to operate the harness. It's different from the ones in the main cabin, causing my fingers to fly around uselessly as I frantically try to pull the straps over my body.

"Here," Enrique says, his tone still harsh but not as loud.

His touch is surprisingly gentle as he pushes my hands away. He leans over and tugs the various buckles into place, the snapping sounds barely registering over the thunderous claps shaking the jet.

"I have no idea where this storm came from," he tells me. "It's like it just magically appeared out of no—"

Boom!

My hands fly to cover my ears, my body trembling as violent vibrations jostle me in my seat.

Enrique curses and starts pulling up various screens showing infrared camera feeds. I try to see what he's seeing, but I don't understand it. However, I grasp that we're in trouble when he freezes at whatever he finds.

He clicks his headset. "Sven?"

My wolf hearing engages, yet nothing but static reaches my ears.

"Elias? Ander? Kazek? Can anyone read me?"

More static.

"Fuck, we're going down," he whispers, the words seeming to be more for himself than for me. "Activate escape pods," he says before I can comment, the demand sending a chill down my spine. "*Shit.*" He yanks off his harness. "Stay here, Caja. I'll come back for you."

I blink. "What?"

But he's already out of the cockpit and shouting orders at the Omegas in the back.

"You take pod A," he tells one of them. "You go to pod B. There's no time for me to provide directions, just

77

follow the instructions inside. It's all automated, and from what I can tell, the pods weren't impacted by the lightning strike."

Lightning strike? I repeat, another shiver traversing my spine.

"I'm so sorry," I hear Hel say. "I… I don't know what happened…"

I frown. *Why is she apologizing?*

She mutters something else I don't hear because another *boom* echoes in my ears. I wince, my sensitive hearing not doing me any favors right now.

"Can you control it?" Enrique asks her, his voice a distant rumble that I can barely make out over the reverberations in my head. I've clearly missed some key part of their conversation, though, because I have no idea why he's asking her that.

"N-no…"

"Then you're going in pod A," he replies. "We can't risk another bolt to the jet, and we need you far away from the others so they have a chance of surviving."

My eyes widen. *Does that mean Hel… did this? Is that why she looked so off earlier?* I noticed her paling complexion after takeoff but thought maybe it was just the plane or the fear of the unknown bothering her. Was it something more?

"Okay," she agrees as another sequence of deafening explosions rattle the cockpit.

I try to look behind my chair, to see what's happening, but the straps cut into my chest, preventing my movement. And I have no idea how to unfasten them.

Trembles rack my body at the realization that I'm *trapped*.

Enrique left me here.

No. He's coming back. He... he won't leave without me. Right?

But as a series of *whooshing* hits my ears, I realize the pods are all being deployed, and I'm still here. Strapped in. Facing a wall of darkness sprinkled with flashes of light.

A storm.

And there's blaring happening all around me, too. Alarms. Screens flickering with exclamation points. An automated voice issuing a countdown.

Oh, Gods, I'm going to die here. I'm going to—

"*Caja.*" Enrique's growl rumbles through my mind, jolting my focus up to where he stands beside me. I have no idea how much time has passed, but he has on some sort of backpack, as well as a pair of goggles on his head. "We're going to have to jump."

I blink at him, sure that I heard him wrong.

But as I look out the window, I realize we're no longer in the storm cloud. It's clear again, the moon high up in the sky. Except it's too high. And we're angling downward.

"The jet is going to crash," he goes on. "That freak storm Hel created took out a—"

He stumbles as the cockpit rattles, the vibrations near violent.

"We have to go right fucking now," he snarls, diving forward to rip the restraints off me.

He yanks me out of the seat before I have a chance

to move and starts wrapping more straps around me. Only these ones are connected to him, not the chair.

I cling to his broad shoulders as the ground shakes beneath me, my limbs quaking with nervous energy.

"I've got you," he says, lifting me off the floor. "I promise I won't let go."

He tucks me into his chest, his arms resembling steel bands around me, his strength more secure than the fabric he just wove around my body.

"Close your eyes, Caja," he whispers against my ear before air rushes into the cabin. I bury my head against his chest and cling to him, my heart thundering against my rib cage.

Then the sensation of falling has me screaming in terror, the icy wind whipping around my exposed skin.

Enrique purrs, his rumble loud and demanding as the air ripples around us. I try to press myself into him even more, determined to have that soothing vibration follow me to my death.

Because I have no doubt I'm about to die.

Wolves can endure a lot, but we just jumped out of a jet. There's no way we'll be able to survive this fall. We'll shatter upon landing. Break into a thousand pieces.

But if I have to die, at least it's like this—in the arms of the first caring Alpha I've ever met.

A morbid acceptance. However, I've always known I would die a horrible, painful death. I'm just happy not to be alone.

I relax into his embrace, thankful for his power, his tenderness, the few moments of peace he gave me. "You're a good Alpha," I tell him, uncertain of whether or not he can actually hear me over the roaring wind. "Thank you for showing me that some Alphas can be kind."

A vision of what could have been forms behind my eyes, providing me with a destiny I would have craved in another life. A destiny involving Enrique. Choosing him as my mate. Being claimed by him. Bearing his pups.

It's a dream.

A fantasy I know will never happen.

But it's a nice vision to entertain on the way to my—

His arms shift and everything jolts, eliciting a scream from me as our free fall momentarily jerks upward. And suddenly we're coasting through the air, not free-falling. I blink against his chest, confused by the varied sensation, my stomach rolling in response.

"This is going to be a rough landing," Enrique rumbles against my ear. "But I still have you, tesoro. Just don't let go of me, okay?"

I have no intention of ever letting go of him, so I just cling to him tighter and revel in his purr. It's soothing. Hypnotic. Almost tranquil.

I can hear his heart thudding beneath it all, the steady rhythm one I strive to match. His presence is calming, his strength reassuring.

The rush of air seems to quiet, perhaps because I'm so utterly focused on Enrique that I can't hear anything else.

Then a *thud* rumbles through us both, followed by Enrique jolting forward into a run.

I startle, confused by the jarring change in sensation.

One moment, I felt like I was floating. And now… now everything is bumpy once more.

Enrique releases a string of profanity, his purr dying beneath his words. "I have to set you down, pequeño tesoro."

I clutch his shoulders, not wanting to leave him, but he's already unfastening the straps around me.

"But I need to get this thing off of me, and I can't do that with you in my arms," he tells me as he tries to untangle my arms from his neck.

A whimper escapes me as he succeeds in overpowering my strength, my wolf curling up inside me in terror.

Except my feet don't touch air; they touch something soft. Something *grainy*.

Sand, I realize, glancing downward in a startled blink. *What…?*

I look around, my mind slowly deciphering the vision before me.

Gentle waves.

White sand.

Nearly full moon.

Stars.

Animal whispers taunt my ears, causing me to turn toward the junglelike village behind us. I frown at the buildings, all decorated in overgrown weeds and other wildlife.

"Where are we?" I whisper, confused and alarmed and partly… relieved. Because we survived. My focus shifts to Enrique where he's untangling himself from a series of cords. *A parachute*, I realize, some of the last however many minutes—or *hours*—starting to make sense.

We jumped out of the jet.

With a parachute.

"Why didn't we take an escape pod?" I ask on the heels of my other question.

"It was malfunctioning, probably from Hel's storm," he mutters, slicing through the last of the cords with a knife before ripping off his goggles. Then he points at a glowing fire in the distance. "And we just crashed into Exiled Sector. Specifically, Venom Island."

ENRIQUE

THIS IS A FUCKING NIGHTMARE.

Of all the places to crash a plane, it has to be here—in fucking Exiled Sector. I know very little about the islands in this area, just that all of supernatural kind sends their feral and uncontrollable Alphas here to govern themselves.

I felt the barrier on the way in, the hum of electricity that keeps the rabid Alphas from escaping these islands.

Each one is different, supernaturals picking and choosing how they cage their inhabitants.

I can only hope that the barrier I felt ripple across my skin will allow Caja and me to leave.

Assuming we can even find a way off this godforsaken island.

I run my hand down my face, my legs tight from our abrupt landing. Fortunately, my wolfish genetics are already kicking in to help me heal.

It's been a long time since I used a parachute. And it

was only supposed to be me jumping out of the jet—after I placed it on a self-piloted course for Venom Island.

My original plan was to crash the jet as a distraction so I could land safely on the opposite side of the island, find Caja's escape pod, then locate a place for us to hide while we waited for help.

But the final escape pod jammed, thus changing the plan to me jumping out of the jet with Caja in my arms.

The slight delay placed us a lot closer to the crash site than I originally anticipated.

Caja is still staring at it with wide eyes, utterly oblivious to the dangers waiting for her here.

She's an Omega on the verge of her first heat—a heat I only began to sense right as that lightning bolt hit—and stranded on an island full of feral Alphas.

This is about to go really fucking wrong, really fucking fast.

I check my watch. *No signal.*

Of course there's no fucking signal.

We're cut off from everyone here.

Our only saving grace is that Ander will soon realize we never made it to Nova Sector. Then, hopefully, he'll activate his tracking system on the jet and the pods and send a rescue team after us.

If his team can cross that barrier, anyway, I think, frowning. Ander's wolves won't be able to come get us if that magical barricade functions as a one-way entry system. This place is meant to keep the inhabitants inside of it—for good.

But maybe there's a backdoor method I don't know about.

I've never been a Sector Alpha, so I don't know the nuances of this place. I just know I've never wanted to come here.

Well, too late for that. Because we're fucking here now. And...

"We need to run," I tell Caja. "Take off your clothes and shift." Because she will very likely need her teeth and claws.

Her dark eyes blink away from the distant flames to look at me. "Shift?"

"Yes. Now, Caja." There's no time for me to be gentle or to explain. She just needs to do what I ask and let me lead.

I squat to cut another strand, freeing the bag I packed back on the jet. It's full of firearms, grenades, flares, and a few essentials. All of the escape pods should have been stocked with similar items, but there wasn't time to check each one individually. I could only point to the escape pod's automation system, then shut them inside.

And pray they all landed safely.

My gut twists at the idea of all those other Omegas being lost among these islands. I basically just transported them from one hell to another.

Caja called me a good Alpha while in the air.

She has no idea how wrong she is about that. I just lost eight Omegas. *Eight.* That's not the mark of a good Alpha.

I should have been paying better attention, realized

something was going on, and helped Hel before her power imploded.

Granted, I have no idea what I should have been looking for. She was an Ulv wolf. I didn't even know they possessed the ability to control the weather.

Shit. I scrub my face again, then shake my head. There isn't time to dwell on this. I may not have been able to save all the Omegas, but I do have one I can protect. And I'm going to do everything in my power to ensure she survives here.

I spin toward her and still as I find her jet-black wolf sitting on the beach, gazing up at me obediently.

She's so fucking pretty. All I want to do is go down on my haunches and nuzzle her soft-looking snout.

Instead, all I say is "You're beautiful." Because I can't *not* say anything. She's *stunning.*

But rather than touch her like I want, I busy myself by bending down, scooping up her clothes, and stuffing them in my pack.

She shakes out her coat in response, then blinks up at me expectantly.

"We're going to run now," I tell her. "I want you to follow me and do exactly what I say when I say it, okay?"

She cants her head, and I translate that as a confirmation.

"Good girl," I praise her, then secure the bag on my back. "Let's go."

Caja trots along beside me while I scan the coastline, my senses on high alert.

Venom Island used to be known as Jamaica, but the once resort-dotted beach has been reclaimed by the wild greenery around it. Like many other areas of the world, it boasts a dystopian flair, telling the tale of what life used to be in this world and what life on this planet has become.

I walk carefully and alertly, listening and searching for threats. I purposely chose Venom Island because it houses the creatures I know—fellow X-Clan Alphas. Much better than the neighboring Outcast Island, a volcanic landscape filled with vampires.

A shudder works through me at the thought.

I really hope Guðrún didn't end up there, but she was in one of the last pods. An error in judgment on my part, but I wasn't paying attention to the order in which everyone escaped. I just wanted to get them all off the jet before it crashed.

There was no way I could have landed it safely. That jet was going down with or without us in it, and I chose the second option.

Caja and I continue down the beach, the moon bright overhead. It's maybe three or four in the morning. I check my watch and confirm that it's just after three.

And I note that the symbol showing we're disconnected from the world is still flashing at the top of my screen.

You know it's bad when satellite tech doesn't work in your location, I think darkly.

Pushing the thought away, I focus on a thick cluster of trees ahead. It's bordering one of the old resort properties, the underbrush thicker than the others. It looks like the beach thins beyond, turning into rocky coastline that starts to curl into a cove.

I pause when we reach it, noting the rapidly increasing elevation. Most of the cove is shrouded in cliffs, not beach, the terrain hillier than I expected for being so close to the water.

But that gives me an idea. The closer we are to water, the easier it'll be to mask Caja's scent. It's why I've been hugging the coastline—in case Caja needs to dive in and wash off her alluring perfume.

"Stay here for a minute," I say, darting into the trees to see if there's a good path to the rocky coastline. What we need is a cave. Preferably one that's hard to access and only has a single entry point—a point I can easily guard.

It takes a few minutes, but I finally locate a path that allows me to better evaluate the cove. I perch up on a rock, surveying for anything promising.

The water bathes the stones, then draws back to the sea, only to rush forward again.

Nothing catches my gaze as a potential hiding place. However, I know there has to be something.

I sit and observe, all the while counting minutes in my head.

Caja isn't far behind me, her scent slithering through the air like a fucking beacon. My cock hardens more and more with each inhale, her heat fast approaching.

We're just going to have to gamble, I decide, picking a darkened location in the distance that appears to have a sunken facade in the rocks. If it's not a cave, we'll—

A howl in the distance has the hairs dancing along my nape, that sound one I know too well.

It's an Alpha alerting his pack.

An Alpha on the hunt.

An Alpha who just scented a fertile Omega.

"*Fuck.*" I sprint out of the woods to where Caja is cowering by the water, her wolf's tail between her legs. "This way," I tell her urgently.

She doesn't hesitate, her wolf leaping to my side to follow me through the underbrush. It's a literal jungle in here, the rocky ground a lot harsher than the sandy beach. But Caja follows me with ease, her wolf agile and small, allowing her to move quickly at my side.

I pick up the pace as the howls grow louder, my inner wolf snarling in response.

Ours, he's saying. *This Omega is ours.*

And we do not fucking share.

"Focus on me," I say, wanting Caja's complete attention. "Ignore their howls."

It's probably easier said than done. Especially for an Omega on the edge of her heat.

All it will take is a growl to make her supplicate and shift back into human form. She's vulnerable to an Alpha's demands even when not in this condition. Add in her estrus, and she's helpless to our call.

She'll roll onto her back and spread her pretty legs, then beg for a knot.

My own knot throbs at the thought.

It's a basic need. A drive to fuck. To claim. To *breed.*

Is that why I've found her irresistible? I wonder, then frown.

No.

She's not the first Omega who has gone into heat around me. I saw Kari through one a year ago, purred for her and forced her to sleep while her body contorted in agony. Never once did I want to fuck her.

And I attended my fair share of estrus parties, too. However, no Omega ever called to me like Caja does now. Maybe because Kari was always my focus, but I would have deviated if someone like Caja caught my attention.

There is just something about her that calls to my inner wolf, demanding that I pursue her.

If she'd been at one of those parties, I would have struggled to pick between Kari and Caja. I would have wanted to select them both for very different reasons.

Kari, I just wanted to save.

Caja… Caja, I want to drag back to my lair. I want to knot her until she can't fucking walk. I want to sink my teeth into her flesh and make her *mine*.

Another howl stirs a responding growl in my chest. It's possessive and feral, and it causes Caja to stumble alongside me.

"Shit," I mutter. "Sorry. It's my wolf. He feels challenged."

Because he is being challenged.

By an island full of feral wolves.

My feet move faster, the need to find somewhere safe for Caja driving my instincts. She runs along with me, but I can feel her anxiety now, smell her fear. It's a fucking aphrodisiac that's going to attract even more predators.

And it's driving my inner beast mad with lust.

I fight the urge to growl and demand that she shift. To take her against a godsdamn tree like a savage.

The crashing of the water against the rocks is the only sound that grounds me in the present, forcing me forward as we run along the interior of the cove. We're on an incline, jogging upward and toward more trees situated along a cliff's edge.

There are no old buildings here, just lush trees and jagged underbrush.

I pause to glance out over the coast, my gaze seeking the space I noticed while searching the area earlier. *Almost there*, I think, taking off again.

But the howls are loud now, the sounds scattering goose bumps down my arms. *Faster*, I tell myself. *Fucking Faster*.

Caja sprints alongside me, her terror mounting.

Then I freeze as an unwelcome scent hits my senses. *Alphas*.

A growl tightens my chest. "*Run*," I tell her, taking off away from the coastline and abandoning the cave plan. Caja follows on my heels, her wolf panting with the effort.

I have no idea where we're heading now, just away from the Alpha scents. Away from the howls. Just... *away*.

I leap over a fallen log and she does the same, then I sprint toward the sound of rushing water. It's inland, suggesting it's either a creek or a waterfall, but maybe it can help hide Caja's scent.

Oh, who the hell am I kidding? Her perfume is like a damn beacon that's screaming, *Fuck me.*

Twigs and leaves snap behind us, confirming we're being pursued. Of course, the snarls and howls already told me that.

Most of them are in wolf form, giving them an advantage over my human body. But I can't fire a gun with my paws.

I duck under a low-hanging branch, then come to a screeching halt as I realize we've just hit a dead end.

Or rather, another cliff.

In the form of a waterfall.

I quickly survey the area, my night vision allowing me to see every detail.

We can't jump; there are too many rocks down below. While we would absolutely survive the fall from this height, thanks to our enhanced genetics, it would take a while to heal.

Shit.

Caja brushes against me, her body vibrating with nerves.

I place my palm on her nape, then cock my head to the side, silently telling her to follow me once more.

We travel the cliff's edge until we find what looks like an old, overgrown path. I start down it, then think better of it and whisper, "You go. I'll meet you down there in the water."

Her eyes tell me she doesn't like this idea, her energy humming with alarm. But like a good wolf, she starts the trek while I crouch to open my pack and pull out a few helpful items.

Most wolves fight in animal form.

In any other situation, I would.

But pride is irrelevant tonight. Survival is all that matters. *Caja's* survival.

Slipping the bag back into place over my shoulders, I move to hide behind a tree.

And wait for the Alphas to come out to play.

CAJA

A GUNSHOT RINGS THROUGH THE NIGHT, THE SOUND ONE I recognize from home.

Sometimes Omegas escaped.

But it was always only temporary.

I duck down on the path, my wolf's ears flattening as I try to determine where the sound came from. Only to hear another soon after. Then a ferocious growl. And *howls.*

So. Many. Howls.

I shiver, my fur standing on end.

Where's Enrique?

Bullets can't kill our kind, just momentarily debilitate us. But that debilitated state could be long enough for someone to cut off a head and permanently kill a shifter.

Is Enrique hurt?

I pause on the steep slope to look up to where we parted ways, uncertainty twisting my gut. *Should… should I go back? Does he need me?*

How could I help? I wonder in the next breath, my stomach twisting at the thought.

I… I have claws and teeth… but I've never fought anyone. And I won't stand a chance against an Alpha, let alone a pack of them.

No.

I need to keep going and do what Enrique said. That's what he told me from the beginning—to do what he says, when he says it.

And he said to go down to the water and hide.

Swallowing, I continue my trek, my wolf's paws digging into the earth to help me balance on this severely angled decline. It's not a cliff, but it's bordered by one.

My wolf peeks over the edge, eliciting a tremble deep within. I've never experienced a height like this before, but I'm not a fan.

Another shot rings out, the echo of it skittering down my spine. Or that's what it feels like, anyway.

Moons, please let Enrique be okay.

I force my wolf to move, our paws quivering against the ground.

I'm nearly to the bottom when an explosion rings out, causing me to freeze.

Roars follow, then a shadow appears at the top of the cliff. It's a massive wolf with dark fur and bright gold eyes.

Those eyes lock on me as his lips pull back in a menacing snarl. I hear it as clear as though he were next to me. Then he tips his head back and howls.

Oh, Gods…

My insides quiver, my stomach clenching even harder.

I scramble the rest of the way down toward the water, suddenly needing to cool down. Because my veins are on fire. And my wolf... my wolf wants to let go. To force me back into human form.

No, no, no, I repeat as I sprint into the lagoon. The chill does little to dispel the heat overwhelming my nerve endings.

It's like an inferno is eating through my very being.

I roll around, trying to calm the roaring flames. But they're all-consuming.

And the growls...

Gods, the growls...

I whine, my wolf disappearing as my human form forces its way out.

A scream rips through my throat, the pain of the shift leaving me helpless and useless in the water.

What's happening to me?

"Move!" Enrique snarls, his mouth suddenly at my ear as his hands grab my hips.

I try to obey him. But I... I can't. It's too much. The howls. The *growls.*

I... I...

A vibration overtakes me as something warm cradles my head. *Enrique...*

He's purring.

He's here.

He's alive.

But the world is spinning. Moving too fast. And I'm still too hot. Too... too overwhelmed.

The purr intensifies, Enrique's arms resembling muscular bands around my torso.

Or I… I think those are his arms.

Before I can truly determine the source of the bands, they're gone. And the purring disappears, too.

"I'll be back for you," I hear him say.

I open my mouth to reply, but a *boom* rattles through every inch of my body, making it impossible to speak.

The world goes completely dark.

Then glitters of moonlight peek at me through the ceiling.

Where am I? I marvel, twisting as much as my stomach will allow. It turns out not to be much because a spasm rings through me, causing me to curl into a ball once more. *Owwwww.*

Tears form in my eyes, watering my vision.

Water, I think, clinging to that word. *There's water… beneath me.*

I… I seem to be on some sort of slippery rock. My hand trails along it, the cool texture a welcome reprieve against my hot fingertips. Some of the flames seem to be dying off, my chest no longer burning with unspeakable heat.

I sigh, my eyes falling closed as I draw indiscernible objects against the rock.

Time passes.

Minutes. Hours. I'm not really sure.

I'm lost in a daze, my limbs falling numb.

Then another pang hits me in the stomach, stirring a moan from deep within.

Gods, it hurts!

Every part of me aches, breathing new life into the fire inside me.

A scream lodges in my throat, my hand covering my mouth. Then I bite down on my palm in an attempt to hold it all in. I've experienced agony before. I know how to silence myself. But Gods, this is unlike anything I've ever experienced.

I roll off the rock, then flail as my body is submerged in chilly water. A gurgling sound bubbles around my ears, my arms moving wildly while my hands search for something to grab on to.

Rock, I think, my nails digging into the surface as I try to pull myself up. Then my knees scrape against more jagged edges under the water, drawing blood. But I don't care, I kneel on the rough surface, my head above water and my arms on the stone I just rolled off of.

Or I assume this is where I fell from.

I blink, some of the surrounding area appearing around me. There's more light now. Not that I should need it; my night vision is usually really good. But there are streams of sunlight coming from far above, illuminating the cave around me.

It's… it's a little oasis.

There are waterfalls trickling in along the walls, splashing into the lagoon I'm now kneeling in.

My insides clench again, but not as violently as before, the water seeming to provide a temporary reprieve.

I shuffle a little to sit on my feet, the water hitting

just above my breasts. It's not deep, at least not where I am.

I suspect it might be a similar depth all throughout this underground utopia, but I don't feel comfortable enough to explore. Who knows when that agonizing sensation will hit me again? And if it is deeper elsewhere, I may drown.

Swimming isn't a talent I ever mastered.

Moving again, I sit down and tuck my knees to my chest, then rest my chin on top. The water covers me from the neck down, providing me with even more relief.

Slowly, I start to feel more like me. More focused. More... aware.

Where's Enrique? I wonder, glancing up at the daylight streaming in again. It's definitely been hours since he left. And I haven't heard anything other than the roaring in my head for a while.

Now, all I hear is the trickle of water.

It's soothing, but not as soothing as Enrique's purr.

"I'll be back for you," he said.

When? I want to ask now. *And where did you go?*

I swallow.

What if he doesn't come back?

I can go a long time without food and water. But... but I'll have to venture out eventually. *If I can even find a way out*, I think, frowning as I scan the walls again.

I don't see an obvious exit.

Am I trapped in here? The hairs along my nape stand on end, my mind recalling the explosion I heard after Enrique promised to return for me. I can't remember what followed, the only sounds ones driven by my agony.

What if he sealed this cave somehow?

What if the rocks fell by accident?

Was it a cave-in?

I bite my lower lip once more, my heart pounding in my chest.

Panicking isn't going to help, but neither is sitting here in this lagoon.

Pushing upright, I take a step, wanting to explore, only for flames to overwhelm me once more. A cry escapes me as my knees give out, and the watery haven instantly engulfs me in its cool kiss.

I shiver, more tears trekking down my cheeks.

What's wrong with me? I feel so weak. So helpless. So… so… *hot.*

My eyes widen.

Heat.

Gods, I'm so naïve.

I'm going into heat.

My Alpha stopped the suppressants earlier this month with the anticipation of delivering me to Alpha Carlos. He wanted my heat to be *explosive.*

And now… now it's finally happening.

In a cave.

On an island in the middle of nowhere.

Filled with growling and howling Alphas.

I curl my legs into my chest and press my forehead to my knees, my breath fanning across the water right below my face.

I'm going to die here, I realize.

Because there's no escaping my fate.

Once my estrus hits, I'll be a mindless mess.

And those Alphas... those Alphas are going to knot me to death.

Unless Enrique returns for me.

If he's even alive...

ENRIQUE

I'M COVERED IN BLOOD AND THE REMNANTS OF DEATH.

Yet hard as a damn brick.

Gods, I'm over a mile away from Caja, and I can still fucking smell her. It's like she's branded my wolf despite being unclaimed.

All I want is to run back to her and fuck her for hours. But I need to finish gathering supplies.

I spent the majority of the early hours fending off Alpha challengers. Several of them are currently trapped in a hole I created with explosives. Lopping off heads was going to take too long, so I crafted a temporary holding solution instead.

A bullet to the brain kept an Alpha down for a few hours, thus allowing me to drag bodies back to the crater and drop them inside of it. They'll eventually find their way out, but by then, I'll be sequestered in the cave with Caja.

Or that's the plan, anyway.

Hence the need for supplies.

Food.

Water.

Shelter.

The old hotels were very handy for my purpose, their supplies surprisingly abundant. Unfortunately, humans perished quickly on most islands, their inability to escape the virus wiping them out in weeks rather than months or years like in other areas of the world.

Iceland was an anomaly, as were other Nordic islands with strong supernatural populations.

But wolves didn't like the heat of the Caribbean, and vampires couldn't stand the sunlight.

Creatures like dragons were the ones who prospered here, but they tended to live in more remote locations of the ocean. I have no idea if they're still around this area or not.

I finish filling a bag—one I found in a closet—with an old skillet, matches, and a towel, then hoist it up onto my back with my other pack. Then I bend to pick up the net of various fruits and vegetables I've picked from the wild. I wanted to catch a few fish as well, but I haven't found any fishing poles.

So I suppose that means we'll be living on a vegan diet for a few days.

At least it'll get Caja through her heat.

I'm halfway down the moss-covered marble hallway when an unexpected scent assaults my senses, one I recognize almost immediately.

Freezing, I slightly rotate to my left. "Francesca?" I breathe, wondering if I'm losing my mind.

Because this is impossible.

Yet, I *know* that citrusy-lime aroma, the undercurrent providing a subtle strawberry sweetness.

"Hey, big guy," she murmurs, her voice unmistakable. "Long time no see."

I turn around slowly, half convinced I'm hallucinating.

Because Francesca is dead.

Or she's supposed to be.

"How is this possible?" I ask, taking in her tall, slender form. Her dark curls are piled on her head in a bun, her light brown eyes as alert as ever. "You're dead."

She snorts. "Isn't everyone on this fucking island?"

I blink. "I don't understand." I'm pretty sure I'm alive. *Unless… unless…*

My brow furrows. *No. I'm definitely alive.*

Because I can still smell Caja. Her alluring perfume is calling to my cock, telling me I'm very, *very* much alive.

"Your face right now is fucking priceless," Francesca muses, strutting toward me. "Probably looks like mine this morning when I found that pit of Alphas you created. Not a great way to make friends on the island, Riq. Alas, I don't think you're going to find many friendly wolves here anyway."

I narrow my gaze, not liking the subtle threat underlining her words. "Yourself included?"

She considers me, her gaze as astute as ever. "Depends on why Carlos sent you here. Did you finally misbehave? Upset the delicate power balance he has in store?"

I stare at her. "Carlos is dead."

Her dark brows rise. "Oh? Since when?"

105

"Since earlier this week." I slowly set my net back down on the ground, the bags slipping from my shoulders. "The Andorra Sector and Winter Sector Alphas took him out."

"And sent you here?" she asks, a hint of wicked amusement tilting her lips.

"No." I fold my arms, her increasing hostility sending off warning bells in my head. "What's going on, Fran?" We used to be friends—more than that on occasion, actually—but I'm definitely not getting friendly vibes from her right now.

It's also been well over a decade since I last saw her.

All these years, I thought she was dead. *Has she actually been here the entire time?*

"You tell me, Riq," she counters, her gaze narrowing. "Why are you here?"

"Did you happen to see the jet I crashed last night?" I offer, not wanting to give her any other details. Especially since we're not alone.

I've picked up two more approaching scents, both of them familiar, but I can't quite place their identities.

"Yeah. Looked like a fancy piece of machinery," she drawls. "Can't imagine the owner of it will be all that pleased."

"No, I doubt he will be." Especially since it had been carrying nine precious Omegas, all of whom are now scattered about Exiled Sector.

"And who is he, exactly?" a masculine voice asks, drawing my gaze to one of the owners of the familiar scent I caught.

Philippe.

Shit.

It's like I'm meeting with past ghosts.

"Carlos?" he presses.

"I just said Carlos is dead," I tell him, aware that he absolutely heard me say that to Francesca.

"And you expect us to believe you?" a third person asks, the masculine tone making my wolf growl inside.

Xavier.

He tried to kill Carlos thirty years ago. He lost. He *died.*

Yet his blue eyes are bright with challenge as he steps through the hotel's front entrance to join us all in the main hallway.

What the fuck is going on here?

I'm surrounded by three supposedly dead Alphas.

They're all staring at me intently, their vibrant gazes seeming to see right through me.

These three are not like all the Alphas I took on overnight. They're intelligent. Completely coherent. And very ready to accept a challenge.

This is not good. Not good at all.

Caja is out there—alone—and about to go into heat.

I don't have fucking time to address past grievances.

Yet here we are.

"He looks surprised to see us," Francesca notes, her gaze narrowing in suspicion.

"That's because I am surprised to see you," I tell her through my teeth. "What the hell did you expect? I thought all of you were dead." I glance at Xavier. "I watched you fucking die." My focus swings to Philippe.

"And I haven't seen you in over fifty years. Where the hell have you been?"

"Here, obviously," he drawls, his brown gaze sweeping over me. "It's where Carlos sends everyone who opposes him."

"But they've never arrived via a rocket before," Xavier adds, suspicion coloring his tone.

"It's a jet," I correct him. "From Andorra Sector."

One black brow lifts. "From Andorra Sector?" he repeats.

I unfold my arms. "If you search the remains, I'm sure you'll find something that confirms where it's from."

He says nothing, just continues to study me.

"Why do you smell like an Omega?" Francesca asks, having moved closer to me without me realizing it. She's only a few feet away now, her lithe form more catlike than wolflike.

Philippe steps forward, his nose twisting. "It's the same scent I caught on the beach."

"Matches the one on the jet, too. But there were more on the jet," Xavier says, taking a step forward. "You'd better start talking, Enrique."

"Or what?" I challenge, my wolf snarling inside.

Xavier might be an impressive Alpha, one who almost bested Carlos, but I've grown since we last met. I'm strong. And I won't go down easily.

Especially with Caja in the balance.

"There are over thirty Alphas on this island from Bariloche Sector," Francesca interjects, her startling sentence causing my eyes to widen as I return my attention back to her.

"*What?*" I gape at her. "How is that even possible?"

"A lot of Alphas opposed him," Philippe says, sounding bored. "But you never fell into that category, *General.*"

I snort. "You were a general, too." At least until he fell for an Omega and tried to claim her.

His eyes narrow. "Why did he send you here?"

"Maybe he bit one of the Omegas?" Francesca suggests. "That would explain why he smells like one."

"Let him answer," Xavier interjects, his stance widening as his folded arms flex across his chest.

He's a big Alpha.

Bigger than me.

But his little muscle display doesn't intimidate me.

"Tell us why you're here," he says, reiterating Philippe's question. Only, Xavier's version of it is underlined in unquestionable demand.

There's no way I'm going to best the three of them together, not if they choose to attack me.

I may be able to outrun them, though.

But then I can't return to Caja. And she needs me.

Gods, she's on the verge of her heat. I'm surprised these three can't smell it. Maybe it's just ingrained in my nose, her presence claiming my very soul before I've even had a chance to bite her.

Because she's mine, I think, my eyes closing as I inhale deeply.

When I open them again, Francesca is just a foot

away, her eyes nearly level with mine due to her impressive height.

"Just answer the question, Riq." She infuses a gentle note in her tone, one I've only ever heard her use in the bedroom. It's seductive.

And it does nothing for me.

"Bariloche Sector no longer exists," I tell them all. "The Alphas from Andorra Sector, Winter Sector, and Norse Sector burned it all to the ground. Carlos right along with it. And I helped."

Xavier arches a dark brow. "Helped how?"

"I provided security protocol details and killed several of Carlos's generals. Then I watched as Sven Mickelson put a bullet through Carlos's brain. And later, I observed him removing Carlos's head from his body." He didn't burn it, though. Instead, he stuffed it into a box and said it was a gift for Kari.

My jaw flexes, my need to get to Caja building with each passing second.

"That doesn't tell us why you're here," Xavier says, a growl in his tone.

"Part of dismantling Carlos's operation involved moving all the Omegas to other sectors," I growl right back at him. "I was piloting a jet full of Omegas, and one of them—an Ulv wolf—lost control of her abilities and created a lightning storm that struck an integral part of the jet. Everyone jumped into escape pods, and I crash-landed the jet here."

The three of them exchange looks.

"You can believe me or not," I go on. "But I chose Venom Island because it's full of X-Clan Alphas. Not because I knew any of you were here. I just thought it would be better to face feral beings of my own kind than other supernaturals."

Francesca takes a step back, her attention on Xavier. "He smells truthful to me. And trust me, I know when he lies."

I grunt. "I've never lied to you, Fran." She was one of my best friends, once upon a time.

Her lips curl. "Exactly."

I roll my eyes. "You're just as squirrelly as ever."

"You missed me, huh?" she teases.

"No," I say, purposely lying.

Her smile widens. "Now *that* was a lie." She looks at Xavier again. "He loves me."

Xavier doesn't look nearly as amused as Francesca does.

And Philippe… his expression is hard.

"Who were the other Omegas on your jet?" he asks me, the drawl no longer coloring his tone. He's more intent now. Serious. And very much on edge.

"They were Omegas of various origins," I tell him. "All of them recent additions to Bariloche Sector. Young. After your time." Because I suspect he's only asking for one reason—to locate the Omega he desired long ago.

Did he actually mate her? I wonder, my nostrils flaring. *He doesn't smell mated.*

Except…

I breathe in again. There's an underlying hint of apple altering his spicy scent, one I nearly missed. But it grows stronger with every inhale.

He mated her, I realize. *He mated one of Carlos's Omegas.*

"Where did the other Omegas go?" he asks, his wolf flashing in his irises.

"How are you lucid?" I counter, running my gaze over him. "My brother's a feral mess right now, thanks to Carlos's bullshit. But you…" *You're fine*, I almost say aloud.

Only, Philippe isn't fine.

I can see it now in his eyes, the way his inner beast is clawing at him from the inside.

"Shit," I breathe, running a hand over my face.

"*Where* are the others?" he demands, his voice deeper now, more gravelly.

"Philippe," Xavier warns, his dominance underlining the other Alpha's name.

"Andorra," I tell Philippe, ignoring Xavier. "All of the hurt Omegas are in Andorra where an Omega doctor is administering treatment."

Philippe is practically vibrating. "Don't lie to me."

"I'm not lying," I promise. "Andorra has a lot of advanced technology. I've seen it with my own eyes. They cured Kari after what Carlos did to her. And they're helping the other Omegas right now. If you search your soul, deep down, you'll sense the truth." Because his link to whatever Omegas is his should confirm everything I'm saying.

"Who is Kari?" Xavier asks.

"Carlos's daughter," Philippe says through his teeth. "She was barely a girl when I left."

"A lot has happened since then," I mutter, running my fingers through my hair. "Joseph mated Savi."

Philippe stares at me. "He's not here."

112

"I know. Carlos kept him in a dungeon with all the others." I glance at Xavier and Francesca. "Well, I thought he did, anyway."

But over thirty Alphas are here? I think, recalling what Fran claimed. *Which Alphas? Do any others have mates?*

I'm about to ask when a harrowing howl reaches my ears, the source of it piercing my heart.

Fuck.

It's Caja.

And she's in trouble.

CAJA

He's not coming back.

Stop that, I think, trying to push that negative voice out of my head. But it won't stop whispering cruel things.

Enrique's dead.

He left you here.

You're going to die alone.

I bury my face in my knees, my eyes burning with unshed tears. I hate that voice. *Hate* it. Because it reminds me of back home. Back with my Alpha, when he would forget about me for days. Leave me in the basement. Withhold food and water.

Enrique isn't Bautista.

I know this.

I'm certain of it.

But I… I don't know if Enrique is alive.

"I'll be back for you," he promised.

114

He wouldn't say that if he didn't mean it. However, that doesn't mean he can come back.

Oh, Gods…

I run my fingers through my hair, yanking on the strands.

The water around me has started to feel warmer, my body seeming to exude heat. Or maybe it's the streaming sunlight warming the lagoon.

Please keep me cool, I beg. *Please don't let me burn.*

My prayers go unanswered as a wave of hot lava sears me from head to toe, my body trembling violently in response. I bite back a cry, my insides churning with foreign energy.

Gods…

It burns.

I… I can't…

I sink my teeth into my palm, determined not to make a sound, but it's too much, it's… it's *all-consuming.*

And I'm alone.

Enrique isn't here.

He isn't coming back, that evil voice whispers.

"Shut up!" I yell at it. "Shut up! Shut up! Shut up!" The final word leaves me on an agonized scream, one that echoes off the cavern walls.

I grab my hair again, scarcely aware of my blood-slicked palm. I really bit myself. *Hard.* But I can barely feel it.

The inferno bursting inside me is so much more powerful.

So *profound.*

My limbs shake, my stomach churning once more.

I. Need.

But I don't understand what I need. It just *hurts*.

I squeeze my thighs together, a whimper escaping my lips.

Gods, it's hot between my legs. So tingly. So… so… *wet*. And it has nothing to do with the water in the lagoon.

I shiver, my hand creeping downward to palm myself where the heat is most intense. I moan at the contact, my little bundle of nerves practically pulsating beneath my touch.

I never do this.

I was always told not to, that I wasn't allowed to stroke myself.

But I can't help it right now. I *need* this.

I need Enrique.

My Alpha.

My… my *mate*.

Except he's not my mate. He hasn't bitten me.

But oh, I don't care! I want him right now. My wolf is practically demanding his presence. She forces my jaws to open, and a guttural howl escapes my throat.

It's so loud. So terrifying. So *needy*.

Please, I beg Enrique with my thoughts. *Please come back.*

Another howl leaves me, this one filled with agony as I tumble to my side in the water. Only to splash around as I try to resurface again.

Gods, I'm a mess.

I… I can't… I can't stay here.

I swim-crawl back to the rock, my slick palms

making it almost impossible to pull myself out. But somehow I manage, my body instantly burning up without the water.

I curl into a ball, every inch of me engulfed in flames.

Enrique... Enrique... Alpha... Please...

Cries litter the air, the sounds mingling with moans.

And followed by *growls*.

I freeze.

Those growls don't belong to Enrique. They... they belong to... to other Alphas.

Oh, Gods...

I can hear them coming for me. Howling. *Prowling* nearby.

I can smell their intrigue, their masculine traits, their *dominance*.

My thighs clench. *No, no... I want... I want Enrique...*

But I can barely picture his face now, all my instincts demanding satisfaction. A knot. *An Alpha.*

No, I whisper. *No!*

More howls.

Intense growls.

Silent whimpers.

Some part of me knows I need to be quiet, to hide. But it hurts so much to *move.*

Back to the water, I think dizzily. *Drown my scent.*

It hurts to move, to roll, but I... I... *Gods...*

Coolness splashes over me, causing me to still once more. *Can they hear me?* I wonder as I submerge myself in the water. It's a temporary reprieve, granting me momentary sanity as I push back up to the surface.

It won't last long.

I can feel the Alphas coming for me.

Hear their claiming howls.

They're going to rip me apart, I realize, curling my legs up to my chest like I did before. *Gods, Enrique… If you're alive… Please… Please come back for me…*

I close my eyes, determined to see him in my mind. To picture his perfect face.

We only had a few minutes together, but they were enough.

They have to be enough.

I tuck my head and breathe, focusing on him and his scent, all while listening to the males outside.

They're searching. Hunting. But they haven't reached me yet.

It's only a matter of time.

I cover my mouth with my palm, refusing to cry out, refusing to give in to the urge to howl. I have to be strong. I have to wait.

He's coming for me, I tell myself. *He's… he's alive… and he's coming for me. Just be strong… hold on… and don't make a sound.*

ENRIQUE

"THAT MUST BE THE OMEGA CAUSING ALL THESE issues," Francesca muses, her nose in the air. "Been a long time since I smelled something so sweet."

"Who is she?" Xavier demands, ignoring Francesca's commentary, his gaze on me.

"*Mine*," I tell him, ready to tear right through him if I need to.

He inhales, his lips curling with challenge. "Not quite, Enrique. You haven't claimed her yet."

I growl, low and deep. "She's *mine*." And I'll fucking shred him apart if I have to. "Now move."

Because he's blocking my way.

Hell, they're all blocking my way.

Francesca at the front. Xavier to one side. Philippe on the other.

I could run backward, but the hallway leads deeper into the hotel and I want *out*.

Caja screams again, causing my blood to go cold.

I take a step forward, only to be shoved back by Francesca. "Who is she?" she demands.

"Bautista's daughter," I snarl at her. "She's not even twenty. You don't know her."

"And she's chosen you?" Xavier asks, his tone exuding incredulity. "Or did Carlos choose you for her?"

I growl again. "He's fucking dead. And yes, she chose me. She's calling for me right fucking now!" I can feel it in my soul, my wolf dying to go to her. To help her. To *protect* her.

Gods, she's too far away.

And these assholes won't fucking move!

"Prove it," Francesca dares me. "Prove all of it."

"How the hell would you like me to do that?" And she'd better not suggest I take her to Caja. No one is going near her but me.

Although, another howl has me worried someone else has already found her. Because that howl doesn't belong to Caja, but to another wolf.

I used a grenade to create a cave-in near an entryway within the cavern I left Caja in overnight. The crumbled rocks blocked the path to her location inside. My plan was to dig my way in after returning, which someone else could do if they knew where to look.

Just the thought of it has me taking another step, only to be shoved back again.

"Call Andorra Sector," Fran tells me.

I gape at her. "*What?* How the hell would you like me to do that?"

She points to my watch. "With that."

I lift it up for her to see. "There's no connection."

She grins. "Yeah, I can fix that." She looks at Xavier. "Flip it on."

"I don't answer to you, Fran."

She rolls her eyes. "Just do it, X. If Riq here is telling the truth…" She lets the sentence hang, the two of them engaging in a battle of wills between their gazes.

All while the howling grows in the distance.

Definitely Alpha male howls.

"I don't have fucking time for this," I snarl, pushing past Francesca—something that's easy to do this time since her attention is on Xavier.

Except she grabs my arm, her claws digging into my flesh.

"Don't," she warns me as Philippe steps into my path.

"Caja needs me," I say, my voice lethally quiet. "I'm going."

"Make the call," Xavier says to my back.

I spin toward him. "For the last fucking time, I—"

He grabs me by the neck and shoves me into a wall, his weight pinning mine as he slowly repeats, "*Make the call.*"

I push him off of me, my wolf itching for a fight. My fist sails through the air in an arc toward his jaw just as my wrist begins to buzz, causing me to falter mid-punch.

My knuckles still make contact, but not with as much force as I intended, and I jerk my hand back to look at my watch.

Xavier comes at me, but Fran body-slams him before he can make a connection. Philippe steps forward like he's about to take over for Xavier, but he freezes as a screen populates the air before me.

"Where the hell are you?" Ander demands before I can speak. "I've been trying to reach you for hours."

Yeah, and somehow his call just came through.

Probably because of whatever Xavier *flipped on*.

"Venom Island," I mutter, somewhat surprised he doesn't know that already. His jet should have provided my coordinates.

"Venom Island?" he repeats incredulously. "Why the fuck are you on Venom Island?"

I blow out a breath, my wolf pacing inside me with the need to get to Caja. But I can't do that if these assholes won't let me fucking leave.

So I'll give them the *proof* they want.

But to do that, I have to answer Ander's question. "Hel had some sort of magical episode on the flight and created a freak storm."

He stares me down over the screen, saying nothing.

"The Omegas took the escape pods," I add. "I… I don't know where any of them are except for Caja."

"Caja's with you?" he asks after a beat.

"She's…" I trail off. "She's on the island."

He frowns. "I don't like the way that sounds, Enrique."

"Trust me when I say I don't either," I growl, wincing as I hear her howl in the distance. "Can you track the escape pods to see where they landed?"

His jaw flexes on the screen. "No. Everything went dark when you crossed into Exiled Sector. I don't know if it's the storm you mentioned or something with the island barriers, but we lost sight of everything and everyone several hours ago."

"Fuck," I breathe, my heart pounding in my chest. I was relying on Ander's fancy technology to be able to save the others. But if he can't even track them…

"We also only have jurisdiction in Venom Island," he goes on. "So if they landed anywhere else, which it sounds like they have, we would require outside assistance. But without coordinates…"

"You have no idea where to start," Xavier interjects as he steps up beside me, his knuckles brushing the blood from his busted lip.

Ander's gaze widens, recognition flashing in his features. "Xavier?"

The Alpha in question notches his chin upward. "Been a long time, Cain."

"No shit. What the hell is going on there?"

"A whole hell of a lot," Xavier tells him.

Ander studies him, frowning. "Things look to be a bit rough there, Xavier."

He grins in response, his tongue touching the wound I created before he replies, "Enrique was just auditioning for a position in the Venom Island hierarchy."

I grunt. "I want no such position."

"Too bad, Riq, you have one hell of a punch," Francesca murmurs. She comes to stand beside Xavier. "I think you have your proof, X. Let Riq go to his Omega."

Xavier narrows his gaze. "We're not done talking."

A chorus of howls punctuates his statement, causing my jaw to clench.

"I don't fucking care if you're done or not," I tell Xavier, taking off my watch and handing it to him. "Chat for as long as you like. I have an Omega to hunt."

"Enrique," Ander calls after me as I push through the crowd to retrieve my bags. "Elias is already on his way."

"Good," I say. "I look forward to seeing him."
Assuming I survive whatever's waiting for me near Caja's cave.

"How's he going to get through the barrier?" Xavier asks.

I'm barely listening as Ander softly says, "I think you and I have a lot to talk about, Xavier."

"I think we do, too," he replies. "Starting with the Omegas you've supposedly rescued because I have a bunch of Alphas on this island with missing mates."

I walk by as Ander nods in response.

Francesca falls into step beside me, announcing, "I'm going with Riq. Meet you at base in an hour, X."

"I don't need you to come with me." Nor do I want her to accompany me.

"Oh, yeah, you do," she drawls. "Because those howls? They're from the rogues. And you're going to need some help taking them out."

I start jogging as soon as I hit the doorway. "I did just fine last night."

"Yeah, with the broken mutts on night shift," she says. "Those idiots get spooked by their own shadows. The rogues, however, have their wits about them. They're feral. Deadly. And very hard to kill."

I glance at her. "And I'm supposed to believe that you're going to help me?"

She shrugs. "What other choice do you have?"

"Maybe I'll throw you into that hole with the *mutts*," I say.

She smiles. "Try and I'll take you right down there with me, Riq."

I shake my head and take off at a sprint toward the place where Caja is hiding.

Francesca is right—I don't have a choice but to let her follow. That doesn't mean I'll rely on her help, though. It's been far too long since I last saw her. And I'm not naïve enough to trust her, history or not.

But I am glad Xavier and Philippe are distracted by Ander. The fewer Alphas I have to deal with, the better.

My senses sharpen as we run, my wolf listening for Caja. She hasn't screamed recently, her last howl maybe ten or fifteen minutes ago at best.

Too long, I think. *It's been too long.*

I don't like that she's silent.

I also don't like the masculine howls growing louder with every step.

They've definitely found Caja. The question is, have they reached her?

A triumphant howl echoes in the daylight, the sound an ominous response to my query.

I run faster, my pulse pounding in my ears. *If I don't make it in time, I'm going to rip everyone apart on this fucking island,* I vow. *Including Xavier, Philippe, and Francesca.*

"Is there a reason we're not shifting?" Fran calls as she keeps pace right behind me.

I ignore her.

She'll find out soon enough.

I don't slow until we close in on the waterfall. It's about a hundred yards ahead and swarmed with snarling wolves.

I don't think; I act, taking a knee and dropping my packs to the ground.

"Finally," Francesca mutters as she rips off her shirt and starts unfastening her pants.

Then freezes when I pull two guns from my pack.

"Holy shit," she breathes.

"This is why I didn't shift," I tell her, and open fire on the rogues by the falls.

I hit three right in the head before they realize what's happening. Then two dart under the water to hide while four others scramble up the steep incline.

I take all four out in a few seconds, then check my ammunition.

Between last night's antics and this new situation, I'm running low. And I only have one magazine left in the bag.

I pocket it, grab two knives, and start toward the waterfall to handle the other wolves.

"Why the hell did you let us corner you if you had all this on you?" Francesca hisses.

"I wouldn't say I let the three of you do anything," I mutter back at her. "And at close range, you would have stopped me before I had a chance to grab the gun from the pack. It also would have given away my advantage."

A wolf growls from the top of the falls, drawing my

focus upward. I aim, pull the trigger, and watch his body fall off the cliff.

"Jesus, I forgot how good a shot you are," she says, sounding a little breathy.

"Still think I needed help?" I ask her as we walk toward the waterfall and the cavern behind it.

"And as cocky as ever, too," she muses.

"Not cocky, just determined." I press my back to the wall near the water, my senses searching for the rogues on the other side of the falls.

Only, a sharp scream distracts me from everything— and everyone—else.

My Omega.

I run toward the sound, my heart in my throat.

If they touch her… If they knot her… If they claim *her…* I'll never forgive myself.

"Riq!" Francesca shouts, but I'm too locked in on Caja to really hear her.

I'm running. *Sprinting.* Solely focused. *One goal in—*

Sharp teeth clamp around my neck as claws take me to the ground, my world flipped upside down.

A broken snarl rattles my chest, my windpipe crushed by a set of heavy jaws.

The gun in my hand almost slips, but muscle memory clicks into place as I point and pull the trigger.

The beast yowls in response, releasing my neck, and I quickly add a bullet to his head. A second rogue lunges for me, and my movements are slow, but I manage to send a bullet into his shoulder.

Then a big black wolf tackles him to the ground.

Francesca. Her teeth clamp into his throat and rip it clean off of him in one yank.

In the next instant, she does the same to a furious gray wolf. One pounce, a single bite, and his neck is twisted at an awkward angle.

Good fucking thing she wasn't the one who caught me unawares, I think dizzily, my throat still wounded.

I can't breathe.

But I can hear my Omega crying for me.

She's nearby.

So close.

"Enrique," she's saying, her voice catching on a sob. "You came back…"

Of course I came back, I think at her. *You're mine.*

I try to find her with my gaze, but everything around me exists in shades of black.

Fuck. I'm losing consciousness.

It'll be temporary. I'll heal. I just hope… it'll be… fast enough.

CAJA

A BIG BLACK WOLF STARES AT ME THROUGH THE RUBBLE, its head cocking to the side.

The gray wolf that was digging through the rocks has disappeared. He was almost through, the hole he created more than big enough for me to squeeze through.

But I don't move.

Because that big black wolf is still studying me.

It smells different from the others. Less hostile. I frown. *Feminine.*

I've never met an Alpha female, but I'm pretty sure that's what this wolf is.

She confirms it by changing back into her human form, her skin the same color as her wolf's coat. "Caja?" she asks.

I swallow. "Who are you?" My voice comes out scratchy.

"Francesca," she says. "An old friend of Enrique's."

I blink at her. *She knows Enrique?*

I can see him just beyond her, his eyes closed, his throat covered in blood. *Is he okay?* I wonder, then whimper as my stomach clenches with discomfort.

Everything still burns.

Terror overcame me for a few minutes when that gray wolf almost made it through, helping to allow sanity to take hold. But it's slipping again.

Gods…

"Enrique," I breathe. He's my anchor. My Alpha. My… my *choice*. He's been so kind to me.

And he came back.

But he's no longer conscious.

"Caja," Francesca says again. "Can you come out of there? We can't stay here."

I blink at her and shake my head. I'm not leaving this lagoon. Not until Enrique is… is… Not until he tells me to.

"Please?" she presses. "Enrique is going to wake up any minute, but he'll need you ready to run. Can you shift?"

I shake my head. There's no way I can let my wolf out right now. Not in this state. Not when everything is so *hot*.

The second I leave the water, I'll be on fire again.

"It's… okay," I hear Enrique grate out, his voice scratchy. "Fran… won't hurt you, tesoro."

I perk up at his nickname for me, my wolf practically sighing inside.

"He'll be good as new in a minute," Francesca adds. "He just made the mistake of forgetting how to be a wolf."

Enrique makes a strangled sound that I think might be a grunt.

I'm not sure where he found this Alpha or how well they know each other. But Francesca seems rather fond of him. A little too fond.

My wolf grumbles inside, sensing potential competition.

I don't like it.

I don't like it at all.

"Did you just growl at me, little wolf?" Francesca asks, sounding amused.

I narrow my gaze, not at all appreciating her condescending tone.

"You did," she says with a laugh. "That's cute."

I snarl. *It is not fucking cute.*

She chuckles again. "Chill, little wolf. I have a lock, not a knot."

"I don't think that's why she's growling," a new voice muses from nearby. "You're competition, thereby a different kind of threat."

Francesca snorts. "Trust me, there's no competition. Enrique's positively enamored with this one. Fucking went through the waterfall without even checking for potential threats, all because he heard her scream. I was super impressed with his skills... until that moment."

A face appears in the hole, the owner of it male and very much an Alpha. "Hi, sweetheart," he says to me, making me flinch away from him. "Don't worry, Omega. I'm happily mated. I just came by to give you all a ride."

"X sent you?" Francesca asks. "I told him we'd meet him at the compound in an hour."

The Alpha shrugs. "He said you might need a lift back to the compound."

Francesca grins. "He's always worrying about me."

"It's his job," the male drawls.

"So he says," she replies, standing up. "By the way, Enrique, this is Hawk. He's from Cusco Sector. Hawk, the shy beauty in there is Caja."

I shiver as he looks at me again, his eyes seeming to shift color with every movement. Or maybe it's the flickering light above.

Another tremble works through me as my stomach convulses, my insides stirring a fresh wave of heat. I swallow a moan, my eyes falling closed.

I hear Hawk rumble out something, but the words are lost to the roaring in my ears.

My forehead falls to my knees as the tang of blood hits my senses. *I've bitten my lip.* Yet I don't even feel the residual ache. All I sense is the growing inferno inside me. The… the intense *need* clawing at me from within.

"Caja." Enrique's dominance surrounds me in a warm caress, the command in his voice demanding my attention.

I lean toward him, my gaze opening to find his.

Only, he's behind that wall of rocks.

"Crawl to me, pequeño tesoro," he purrs. "Crawl to me and I'll give you what you need."

My wolf whines.

He's teasing us. Making us work for his affection.

Mean Alpha.

But a growl from him has me longing to obey.

Gods, I'm on fire again. I need him. Want him. *Crave* him.

I'll crawl anywhere he demands so long as he'll touch me.

I must say that aloud because he replies, "Show me, Caja. Show me how good you are."

His words inspire a desire to please him. To *win* him.

He wants me to show him how good I can be? Oh, I'll show him. I'll make him want me as much as I want him. Make him lose his mind the way I'm losing mine.

The rocks bite into my palms as I pull myself out of the water, but I barely feel the sting. My knees are next, the ground no doubt scraping my skin.

Yet all I can focus on is Enrique's darkening gaze. He's watching me like a predator observes his prey. Like he wants to devour me.

I quiver, liking the way he's staring me down.

His wolf is very much present. I see him lurking in his eyes, regarding me with undeniable interest.

Mate, my inner animal seems to pant. *Ideal mate.*

Francesca says something, her feminine voice an unwelcome interruption that causes me to growl.

I swear she laughs again.

But Enrique doesn't even acknowledge her. His gaze is solely focused on me. I preen, pleased with his attention, and make my way through the small opening in the wall in an attempt to reach him.

He growls as I succeed, his hands instantly finding my hips as he yanks me up into his body. "You're so fucking beautiful, Caja," he tells me. "And so fucking mine."

My body tingles in response to his vocal claim. But I need more. So. Much. More.

"You can't knot her here," that female says, making me want to claw her eyes out. She has no part in this discussion. No part in this *anything.* This is *my* Alpha, not hers, and I proceed to demonstrate that by sinking my teeth into his neck.

I only belatedly realize he's covered in blood.

His blood.

Because his throat…

Oh, Gods. I recall watching that wolf attack him earlier. I couldn't see much through the small hole, but Enrique's essence is all over his neck and shirt.

Tears well in my eyes.

He was hurt.

And now I *bit* him.

What is wrong with me? I wonder, shuddering against him. "I… I…" A pang shoots through my lower body before I can form the apology I meant to voice. Instead, a moan escapes me, one Enrique silences with his mouth on mine.

He's kissing me, I marvel. *Oh, moons, he's* kissing *me.*

And for the first time in what feels like a lifetime, I can breathe.

I wrap my arms around his neck and cling to him as he explores my mouth with his tongue.

He's growling. Purring. *Vibrating.*

All Alpha male.

All mine.

His strong arms band around me, holding me to him as those vibrations tremble through both of us.

But it's his mouth that truly captivates me. His tongue. His lips. His *teeth*. He's kissing me to my very soul.

Gods, I've never experienced anything like this. Never even knew it was something I wanted.

I've seen Alphas kiss Omegas before, but never like this. Enrique is tender. Giving. *Sensual*.

The Alphas of my past *took*. This Alpha *gives*.

Those other Omegas always looked lifeless when my Alpha kissed them, like they were dolls, not wolves.

But this Alpha—*Enrique*—makes me feel alive. Animalistic. *Feral*.

I want more.

I want *him*.

And I tell him that by squeezing my legs around his hips.

I have no idea when he lifted me or how I found myself wrapped around him, but I don't care. All that matters is his touch. His mouth. *His skilled tongue.*

His purr intensifies as he moves his lips away from mine to press a series of kisses to my cheek all the way up to my ear. "You're being such a good girl for me," he whispers. "Just hold on a little more, okay?"

I blink, confused by what he means.

Then my eyes widen at the change in scenery.

We're no longer in the cave.

The vibrations I felt… they must have been from him carrying me out of the cave. Because we're outside and the waterfall is nowhere to be seen.

H-how?

My throat works as I try to figure out where we are and what we're doing.

"How far away is the compound?" he asks, his mouth still by my ear.

I frown. *What compound?*

"Fifteen minutes," a male replies. *Hawk*, my memory supplies.

"You'll need to mark her before we arrive," the female adds, making me growl inside. "Otherwise, you'll start a riot among the unmated Alphas. We might be mostly civilized on our side of the island, but your Omega is a beacon for chaos right now."

My growl rumbles through my chest. *I'll show you chaotic*, I think, ready to challenge the female. Because how dare she speak to my male. My Alpha. *My mate.*

"Shh," Enrique hushes me, pressing a kiss to my raging pulse. "You're the only one I want, tesoro."

I rub myself against him, causing his hands to tighten on my hips.

"Keep doing that and I'm going to knot you in the back of this car," he tells me.

Car? I think, my eyes having fallen closed again. I open them once more and take in the massive vehicle beside us. It's a four-by-four like my brothers used to drive out in the country. Just seeing it sends a chill down my spine.

But that chill is quickly replaced by heat as Enrique climbs up into the back while holding me against him with one arm wrapped around my lower back.

So much strength, I marvel, sighing inside. *An ideal Alpha.*

He sits down with me astride his lap and releases his hold on me. I whimper at the loss, then lean firmly into his touch as he cups my cheek. "I need to bite you, Caja."

There are no words necessary. No form of acceptance I could possibly utter. I simply arch my neck and offer every inch of me for him to claim.

I'm his.

I have been since he pulled me out of that cage.

My wolf knew her mate. I recognized him, too.

And now… now he's going to accept that bond. Confirm it. *Solidify it.*

The vehicle roars to life, but I ignore it, my focus entirely on the Alpha beneath me.

"Gods, I can't believe you're about to be mine," he says, a hint of wonder in his voice. "I don't deserve you, pequeño tesoro, but I'm going to spend the rest of our existence ensuring I'm good enough for you."

He leans forward, his mouth finding my neck. Then he moves lower to my breasts, causing my nipples to harden in expectation.

Yes, I think. *Oh, yes…*

Everything is so sensitive.

I want his mouth on me. His knot inside me. His teeth—

I scream as he bites down just above the areola of my right breast, his claim searing and overwhelming and so *amazing*.

My blood hums in response, my wolf sighing at the

fullness touching our soul. *Claimed. Owned. Possessed. Protected.*

This Alpha is ours.

This Alpha chose us.

This Alpha desires *me*.

I can feel his knot pulsing beneath the zipper of his jeans, his body primed and ready to take mine. The notion of it terrifies and excites me at the same time.

I've seen Alphas rut.

I know how dangerous they can be.

But I trust this Alpha not to hurt me.

His mouth finds mine, my blood a lingering taste on his tongue. I suck it off, then kiss him with a vengeance. I have no idea if I'm doing it right. I don't even care. He's *mine*. He'll teach me if he feels I need to be taught. He'll make me his in every way.

His palm leaves my cheek, going to my nape as he deepens our kiss. I press myself more firmly against him, needing more. *Demanding* it. His opposite hand travels between us, making me shudder with that strange mix of excitement and fear.

But rather than free himself from his jeans, he cups me between my thighs.

I jolt as his finger enters me, the sensation so foreign yet so *good* that I can't hold back my moan.

Someone curses from behind me. I ignore them, too focused on my Alpha to care about anything or anyone else.

My sensitive bundle of nerves throbs against his palm, eliciting a cry from me. It's not enough. Yet it feels so, so *good*.

"Fuck, tesoro," Enrique breathes against my mouth. "You're killing me."

I'm not sure what he means, and he doesn't give me a chance to ask because he's kissing me again, his grip on my nape harsh and demanding.

I arch into his touch between my legs, seeking more. Seeking him. Seeking *bliss*.

It's instinctual, my body just seeming to know how to move while my inner wolf drives my desires. I don't fully understand what I'm searching for, what my animal craves. But I'm moving. Chasing the sensation. Feeling it building.

Gods, whatever it is, it's intense.

It's right there.

So, so close.

Enrique must sense it, too, because his movements change, a second finger slipping inside me to join the first.

I pant, his touch making me feel so *full*, yet not nearly full enough.

He gently bites down on my lower lip, then licks away the pain before kissing a path to my ear. "I'm going to knot you for days once we're alone," he tells me. "Fill you with my seed. Take you in every fucking way possible."

Gods, that sounds like a threat and a promise at the same time.

I know what he's saying—that he's going to rut me. I know from watching others that it's going to hurt. But right now, I don't care. I want him to take me, just like he said. I want him inside me. Filling me to completion.

A whimper leaves me, and that female from the front says something. I can't understand her, but Enrique rumbles in response. Then his palm covers my mouth.

"Focus on me, tesoro," he murmurs. "Focus on my touch. My mouth. My *teeth*."

I'm not sure what he means until I feel him nip my pulse.

Then he clamps down, claiming me again, and my world falls apart. It *detonates*. Shatters. Leaving me writhing and screaming in his lap.

Only, his hand muffles the sounds.

Every part of me burns and shakes, the euphoric sensation ripping through my very being.

An orgasm, I realize. *My first time…*

I thought I experienced bliss when I finally touched myself in the water, but this… this is so much more. It's insanity. Pure ecstasy.

And it leaves me quivering on top of Enrique, my body begging for more.

More of what, I don't know.

Him. His knot. His *seed*.

Gods, this is all foreign yet incredibly intrinsic.

I want to mate him. I want him to breed me. *Rut* me.

"Please," I beg against his palm.

"Soon," he promises, his fingers working me into a frenzy once more.

He's added another digit. I don't know when it happened, but I feel it down there, stretching me, completing me, *taunting* me.

I combust again, my back bowing as he keeps his

palm firmly over my mouth. It's maddening. It's rhapsodic. It's *blinding*.

Everything is dark. Then light. Then dark again.

I feel limp. Replete while still strung tight. It's the most bizarre of combinations.

Then we start moving.

Did I pass out? I wonder, confused as I open my eyes once more. We're outside again. Then inside. Surrounded by metallic structures. *A building*.

And suddenly inside a steel box.

It whirs upward, causing my stomach to clench.

Then a masculine voice explains something about codes.

Enrique rumbles a response, his words a blur in my head.

Am I dying? I wonder, my eyelashes fluttering. *Drugged?* No.

It's my heat.

I… I can't really focus.

I know Enrique is carrying me. I feel him. Smell him. *Know* him.

But there are so many foreign scents filling my nose now. Linen. Food. *Is that coffee?*

A cloud suddenly engulfs my being, and Enrique is hovering over me, his dark eyes reminding me of a starless night. "Still with me, tesoro?" he asks, making my lips curl upward.

"I like that name," I tell him groggily, my voice sounding distant to my ears.

He smiles down at me. "I like it, too. It's fitting.

Because you truly are a treasure, Caja. *My* treasure. And I'm about to worship every fucking inch of you."

ENRIQUE

Caja resembles a goddess against the bed, her dark hair splayed out across satin sheets.

When Xavier mentioned a compound, I pictured some place with wired fences and a run-down interior. I couldn't have been more wrong. This place is more like Andorra Sector with all its metallic siding and glass windows. It even has a dome over it.

"Helps keep the rogues and mindless ones out," Francesca explained as we entered ten minutes ago. "And it helps us maintain the climate inside."

"How?" I asked, the word encompassing a myriad of questions—How is this possible? How are you controlling the climate? How do you have a dome? How do you have all these supplies?

"Dragons are not only excellent traders, but they're also exceptionally resourceful" was her response. Followed by, "And the various hotels left a lot of useful materials behind, too."

There wasn't time to ask for clarifications. But I fully intended to question it all later.

After I helped my Omega.

She had passed out after a series of intense orgasms, her head falling to my shoulder.

I carried her into a building—one Francesca explained was usually used to house their dragon shifter visitors—and now I have Caja right where I want her.

Naked.

Needy.

And sprawled out on the bed.

Her swollen lips part as I kiss her jaw, then work my way down her throat to her breasts. I lave the mark I made on her right tit, my wolf purring with pleasure inside.

My female.

My Omega.

Mine.

It's all happened so fast yet feels like over a century in the making.

I've been alone for so long, satisfying my needs through meaningless embraces with Alpha females and a handful of willing Omegas.

That all feels like the distant past now.

Caja is my present. My future. My *life*.

I can't believe she's mine, that this beautiful creature desired me as much as I desired her. I'm so not worthy of her appreciation. But I'm going to make damn sure I live up to her expectations, just like I told her I would.

And I'll start by making her come again with my tongue.

She moans as I suck her nipple into my mouth, her body arching off the bed. I push her back down by settling between her thighs, my elbows braced on either side of her abdomen while I continue sucking on her tits.

Her fingers weave through my hair, her moans vibrating my mouth.

Unintelligible words leave her plump lips, the breathy tones exciting my inner beast.

I did that. I made her pant. Now I'm going to make her well and truly scream.

I'd silenced her before because we were approaching the compound. But Francesca made sure to tell me that these rooms are soundproofed and secure. I set the code just inside the door, ensuring no one can enter without permission.

A good thing, because if anyone disturbs us now, I'll kill them.

I don't even care if we're guests here.

My Omega needs my knot, and I'm going to fucking give it to her. *Hard.* Without restraint. Over and over again.

She shudders, her grip on my hair tightening as I switch breasts.

When I nibble her stiff little peak, she yelps and then moans, her body vibrating with *want.* So I do it again, this time hard enough to draw blood. Because I want to mark her everywhere. Ensure my claim is *clear.*

It's a masculine need.

A savage desire.

But I embrace it.

She practically pants beneath me, my little wolf enjoying my version of pleasure and pain. Every time I nip her, she jolts. Then she groans when I lick her. Cries out when I suck. Screams for more when I start all over again.

By the time I reach the sweet apex between her thighs, she's a mumbling mess of desire-filled pleas.

I lick her delicious slit, sliding my tongue between her slickened folds, and taste every inch of her soaking wet cunt.

It's fucking heaven.

And I tell her that, my wolf very much in my voice as I utter each word. "I'm going to lick you for hours," I warn her. "Eat you for *days*."

Because there's no way I'll ever get enough.

"You taste so damn good, Caja." If innocence had a flavor, it would be this. All vanilla and cream with a touch of residual smokiness.

The type of smokiness inspired by a heat.

"Gods, tesoro," I groan against her clit. "It's like you were made for me."

And maybe she was.

Maybe I was made for her.

I don't fucking know, nor do I fucking care.

I suck her bundle of nerves deep into my mouth and smile when she shatters for me again, her poor little body so primed and ready that it no longer takes much to turn her into an orgasmic mess of pants and screams.

"So fucking good, Caja," I praise her. "You're so fucking good." And I want to reward her.

Which is why I keep licking her.

Sucking.

Nibbling.

Taking her over the edge again and again while my fingers work their magic inside her.

Stretching her.

Ensuring she can handle me.

Because I don't want this to hurt. I want her to feel good. To take my knot with pleasure that never ends.

By the time I'm satisfied with her blissed-out state, she's practically unconscious from the ecstasy rippling through her veins. However, her eyes come alive as I crawl over her and remove my shirt.

She reaches for me, but I push her hand away. "You can touch me after I knot you," I tell her. "Otherwise, I'll explode in your hand, and that's not going to work for either of us."

I'm almost as keyed up as she is, my dick so damn hard that I have to work to ensure I don't accidentally hurt myself as I unzip my pants.

The fabric is coated in blood.

As am I.

But Caja doesn't seem to notice or care. So I don't care either.

I just want to be inside her.

Rut her.

Fuck her.

She whines as I leave the bed to finish shedding my clothes. I growl in response, making her even wetter between her legs, all while reminding her that I'm in charge here. I'm her Alpha. And as her Alpha, I will take care of her.

When I kneel on the bed again, she gazes up at me with eyes that are obsidian in color. I see her wolf. I see Caja. I see *everything*.

And in kind, she sees me.

My pronounced length.

My throbbing knot.

My tightening muscles.

She takes me all in, then licks her lips and spreads her legs in invitation.

I know this is her first time, her first heat, but my tesoro is a natural in bed. She knows exactly how to entice me.

Or maybe it's just her.

My little treasure.

"Gods, I can't wait to be inside you," I tell her as I crawl over her prone form. "It'll hurt, tesoro, but only for a moment. Then I'll make you feel so fucking good that you'll forget your own name."

She stares up at me, her trust-filled gaze making my heart feel like it's about to explode.

This female has fully embraced our mating, relying entirely on her wolf to guide her. And something about that is so fucking endearing that I can't help but pause and admire her inner strength.

I press my lips to hers, praising her with a silent kiss.

Very good, mi tesoro, I think at her. *You're so damn good.*

She can't hear me; our bonds don't work that way. But I know she can sense my emotions, can feel the pride bursting inside me every time I look at her. My admiration. My *devotion*.

And I can sense her returning each emotion in kind.

She trusts me. Trusts *this*. And it's the most precious fucking gift that I can't help but thank her with my tongue.

Her nails dig into my shoulders as I kiss her harder. Then she stills as my cock nudges her entrance. I can't imagine how big I feel to her, my bulbous head nearly the size of her fist.

But her body is made for this. *For me.*

"You'll be okay," I tell her, pressing into her tight entrance. "Just hold on, tesoro. Hold on to me and scream."

Her claws draw blood as I thrust forward, forcing her to take me.

I could go slow, but it would prolong the agony.

This will allow her to accept the burn all at once, to feel my girth as I push myself inside.

She unleashes her suffering against my mouth, her scream ripping me apart and making me still inside her as I allow her a few minutes to just breathe.

I'm not all the way in.

But I'm close.

Tears mar her pretty eyes, her cheeks flushed red with exertion.

"Shh," I hush her, my lips ghosting across hers. "It's okay. You're okay."

She whimpers in response, the sound clawing at my heart.

"I'm sorry, tesoro," I murmur. "I know it hurts."

She quivers, her eyes squeezing closed.

But at the same time, her insides clench around me.

She freezes.

Then does it again, her pussy gripping me like a vise and nearly drawing a growl from my chest.

Because fuck, that feels good.

She's already so damn tight that I'm struggling not to burst.

But now she's massaging my head with her inner muscles, taking me that much closer to the edge.

I reach down to massage my knot, my base nowhere near her entrance since I'm not all the way inside her yet. The sensation of my hand makes my muscles tense, but it allows me to stave off the heat mounting in my veins.

It's been so fucking long since I experienced an Omega's sweet heat.

And the first time I've ever embraced *my mate*.

I'm fucking boiling inside, ready to explode just with that knowledge alone.

That sensation only darkens as she intimately tightens around me again, her little body fucking torturing mine.

"*Caja*," I groan, my forehead going to her neck. "Gods, tell me I can move. Please tell me to move." Because I need to fuck her. To show her how much her body can take. To shove us both into a state of oblivion.

She lifts her hips, taking more of me into her. My fist brushes her clit, causing her to jolt. Then she pumps up her lower half again and moans as my hand comes in contact with her sensitive bud once more.

I release my knot and move my thumb to her little bundle of nerves, stroking her as she welcomes even more of me into the sweet heaven between her thighs.

"Fuck, you feel so good," I praise. "So damn good, Caja."

I'm not going to be able to control myself for much longer.

Because she's fucking killing me here.

Her little body begins to move in earnest, sliding up and down my shaft, taking me as deep as she can from her position beneath me.

When she begins to whimper, I slide a little bit forward and growl when her pussy lips kiss the top of my knot.

"*Tesoro.* Tell me to move. Tell me to fucking move."

She grips my shoulders even tighter as she wraps her legs around my hips. "Take me, Alpha," she says, her voice clear, her eyes even clearer.

Because my Caja is still here.

She's not fully gone to her heat.

Not yet.

But she will be the moment my knot embeds inside her.

Keeping my thumb on her clit, I use my opposite hand to grab her hip. Then I angle her where I want her. "This is going to be hard and fast, tesoro. But I promise I'll make it up to you."

I don't give her a chance to respond before forcing the rest of my length into her sweet little cunt.

She arches and moans, her thighs tensing around me.

Then she screams as I begin to really move.

Pounding her into the mattress.

Claiming her with my body and ensuring she knows exactly who is fucking her.

My name leaves her pretty lips, then I silence her with my tongue and dominate her mouth.

Mine. Mine. Mine.

Every inch of me is staking ownership over every inch of her, just as her soul is possessing my spirit, mind, and heart.

I belong to her.

And now she's going to belong to me.

Every scream. Every orgasmic shudder. Every moan.

I want it all.

I want her.

And I show her that with my hips, my cock, my tongue.

She's panting, crying, growling, and *clawing*.

I'm going to be a bloody fucking mess, and I don't care. Because I'll be her mess and she'll be mine.

My balls tighten, my knot threatening to burst.

It feels so damn good. *So fucking right.*

No one has ever made me this lightheaded with lust, this infatuated with a single look.

Caja is a goddess. My goddess. And I'm going to worship at her altar for the rest of my fucking existence.

I bury my face in her neck and clamp down around her pulse, marking her *again*. Biting her *again*. Ensuring she knows—that *everyone* fucking knows—she's mine.

This female.

This Omega.

This beautiful fucking wolf.

She stops breathing as my knot shoots out of me, her

body freezing against mine, then tumbling into a fit of convulsing paradise as we both fall apart in unison.

Heat blasts through me. Over me. *Into* me.

Ripples of pleasure.

Quakes of intense sensation.

A union defined by our joined passion.

It's so fucking good. Feels so fucking amazing. And it doesn't *stop*.

I growl, my muscles tight as my seed continues to flow into her womb. There are ways to prevent pregnancy among our kind, but I don't have access to any of those tools right now. Nor do I want them.

Because I want her carrying our child.

I want this future.

I want *her*.

And when I pull back to stare down at my Omega, I can tell she wants it, too.

My Caja is still there, blinking in and out of her euphoric state.

"You're mine," I tell her gruffly. "My mate. My Omega. *Mine*."

She exhales, her shoulders seeming to lose a weight I didn't even realize she was carrying. "Thank you," she breathes, her eyes falling closed as she pushes up against me once more. "Thank you, Enrique."

I brush my lips against hers. "No, tesoro. Thank you." Because she's the treasure here. The gift. The one deserving of my gratitude, not the other way around.

But as her eyes open once more, I realize my Caja is no longer with me.

She's fully succumbed to her heat now, leaving a needy Omega behind.

My wolf hums inside, pleased. Because he knows exactly what we're going to do now.

We're going to satisfy our little mate until neither of us can walk.

Then we're going to do it all over again.

And again.

Until her heat subsides.

And once more… when my Caja finally wakes…

CAJA

My Alpha's knot pulses, filling me with his seed. Claiming me. Branding me. *Sating* me.

I bury my face in his neck as he rolls us to our sides, his chest against my back. All while keeping us glued together below.

I'm so full, his cock hard and connected to my insides. I squeeze around him, my inner walls spasming from my ongoing climax.

It just keeps going.

And going.

And *going*.

I start to whine. Or I try to, anyway. My throat is hoarse from screaming. *So. Much. Screaming.*

"Shh," he hushes me. "I need a few more minutes, tesoro."

I shiver, that nickname doing something to me every time he whispers it.

His palm glides down from my hip to my mound, his

fingers gently stroking my clit and sending me over the edge into another cataclysmic downward spiral.

He kisses my neck, holding me while I squirm, his cock still securing us below.

Gods, I feel like he's been inside me for *days*.

And he probably has been.

I have no concept of time. Just heat. Sex. *Cum*.

Ohhh, I love it when he *comes*. It's like he's owning me inside and out.

His teeth sink into my tender skin, not hard enough to draw blood, but enough to make me feel possessed. Claimed. Utterly dominated. And *safe*.

This Alpha protects me. He cares for me. He holds me. *He fucks me*.

His tongue traces a wet path up to my ear where he nibbles the lobe and breathes, "*Mine*."

I shudder, loving that word. "Yours," I agree. "Yours, yours, yours."

"Mmm," he hums. "Such a good girl you are, my sweet little Omega. Do you want a reward?"

I'm practically panting, ready for him to take me again despite his knot remaining inside me. "Yes," I hiss, arching back against him. "Please, Alpha. More."

His finger brushes my clit again, sending me spiraling from that single touch alone. It's like I'm a bundle of nerves, utterly consumed by the pleasure only he can bestow upon my body.

He groans as I clamp down around him, a curse leaving his lips as he buries his head in my neck again, his muscles clenching against my back. "*Fuck*, Caja," he growls. "You're making me want to fuck you again already, and I'm still inside you from our last round."

I wiggle against him, all for his suggestion.

But he stops me by cupping me between my legs and pressing his palm against my sensitive nub.

This time, I don't fall apart. Yet I'm close. *So, so close...*

"No," he growls, holding me as his knot starts to release me.

I snarl back at him, not liking his denial.

"Caja." He nips my raging pulse. "You need to eat."

Ugh. The last thing I want right now is *food.* "I just want your knot."

"And you can have my knot after you eat some fruit," he says, his cock slipping out of me.

I whimper at the loss, my insides already burning up in response to being empty.

I need more.

I need him.

I need my Alpha's knot.

"Food," he reiterates. "We've been fucking for three days, Caja. You need energy. And water."

He pulls away from me, leaving me pouting on the bed.

And eyeing his backside.

He has a seriously nice ass, I think, taking in his naked form. *So sexy.*

He glances over his shoulder. "I think that's the first time I've ever heard you curse, tesoro."

I frown. I must have said all that out loud.

Oh well.

It's still true nonetheless.

"And I think you're sexy, too," he says, winking at me before disappearing from view.

I start to crawl after him, only to pause near the edge of the bed and frown down at the sheets. They're... uneven.

No. No, that's not quite right. They're just not in the correct place.

I run my palm over them to smooth out the texture, but that doesn't seem to help.

Rolling off the mattress, I untuck the sheets and try remaking the bed.

A growl escapes me when that doesn't fix it either.

This is maddening, I think, furious with the bedding. *Why are you so lumpy?*

I yank everything off and onto the floor, then begin again. I'm in the middle of smoothing the edges once more when I feel my Alpha enter the bedroom.

My inner animal vibrates with excitement, ready for our Alpha to pounce. But I hold up a hand. Because I need to fix this first. We can't play in this mess. It's... it's... it's all wrong.

Another growl rumbles through me as I kneel on the mattress and start tugging blankets all over it, trying futilely to fix the wrinkled edges.

My Alpha says nothing.

But then he dares to come near this catastrophe, and I round on him with a snarl, only to see that he's holding a set of linens in his hands.

I blink at it.

Then reach out to run my fingers over the silky texture.

My lips purse. "No." It's too... something. I don't like it.

He nods and leaves me to my task, which is completely hopeless because these sheets are—

"What about these?" he asks while I'm in the middle of rearranging the bed again. I pause and slowly face him, uncertain of what he's holding. But when I see the black linen, my heart skips a beat. It reminds me of his eyes.

I step closer and gently stroke the fabric. It's not as silky as the last batch. It's soft. Like air. Cottony. With a subtle woodsy scent that reminds me of my Alpha.

Did he purposely brush these against his chest? His neck? His groin? All of the above?

If I could purr, I would.

Because yes. Very much yes. I like these.

My Alpha rumbles with approval when I accept his offering. I revel in that sound while I strip off the bad bedding and replace it with the pleasing set.

The edges... are perfect.

No wrinkles.

No unnecessary lumps.

It's... it's heavenly.

But it's still missing something.

Tapping my chin, I search the room and walk over to grab a few pillows. Some of them are good. Some are not.

My Alpha brings me others to test. I select two more, adding them to the headboard, then climb into my nest and fluff the remaining sheets into place.

Pleased, I sigh and relax into the linen.

Only for a pang in my lower belly to cause me to curl into a ball.

"You need to eat," my Alpha reminds me.

No. I need a knot, I think, growling.

"Food, Caja," he says, holding out something sickly sweet. A berry of some kind. I turn my nose up at it, then find my nape caught in his palm.

I growl at him.

He growls back.

Which only has my thighs tingling with want.

"If you eat, I'll reward you," he promises me in that silky voice of his.

My wolf stills at the prospect, causing my mouth to open. He places the fruit on my tongue, and I swallow without chewing. He must notice because he grunts.

I don't care.

I reach for his hard cock, but he pushes my hands away.

"You have to eat more than a strawberry, Caja," he says.

I pout. However, I open my mouth again and swallow as he brings more items to my lips. He keeps the bites small, probably because I'm not using my teeth. Maybe it's petulant, but all I want to do is lick him. Nibble on him. *Suck him.*

My gaze travels back down to his impressive length and the hint of precum on the tip.

I lean forward without thinking and take the offering in my mouth, earning me a groan from my Alpha. His palm is still on my nape, but he doesn't pull me away, just lets me taste him.

"Gods, you're addictive," he tells me, his head falling back as I take him deep into my mouth.

He's been teaching me what he likes, telling me how to swirl my tongue and when to use my teeth. I enjoy doing this to him, watching him lose control, coaxing his beast out to play.

"Fuck, tesoro," he groans, his grip tightening. "I want to take your ass today and lay my claim to every inch of you. But I need to prepare you."

I shiver, not sure what that means, but I like the sound of him claiming me. Marking me. Branding me as his.

He's mine, too.

I remind him of that by releasing his cock and leaning down to nuzzle his knot before gently biting down. *My. Alpha.*

He growls.

I growl back.

And suddenly I'm straddling his face while his hand guides me back down to his cock. "Keep pleasuring me," he demands. "But don't make me come."

That sounds like a challenge.

I like challenges.

Especially sexual ones issued by my Alpha.

I eagerly take him back into my mouth, my tongue doing that thing he likes along the underside of his shaft.

161

But he doesn't curse like he usually does. Instead, he seals his lips around my clit and *growls*.

My legs shake as a fresh wave of wetness—*slick*—dampens my thighs and his face.

He groans, lapping me up and sliding his fingers through my arousal. Except he doesn't enter me. Instead… he brings the slippery essence to my backside and fingers me *there*.

I jolt, realizing what he meant about claiming every inch of me.

He intends to… to… *knot me there*.

Only, I can't take a knot that way, can I?

His palm on my nape squeezes, reminding me without words that I have a job to do—one I've been failing because his opposite hand is distracting me below. As is his mouth. *Gods, his mouth…*

"Caja," he says, a warning in his voice. "Suck my cock, tesoro."

I groan, his demand stirring a fresh wave of need heating my insides and warming my thighs. He licks me deep, then growls against my clit again. I scream in response, the sensation so incredible that I can barely balance on my knees over his face.

His dick pulses against my check, reminding me of his own rising desires.

Taking him into my mouth again, I suck as hard as I can, only to choke as he shoves my head down to swallow more of him.

Precum taunts my senses, forcing my throat to work around him as I try to take every ounce of him in me.

All while he pumps fingers in and out of me below.

Is he using three now? Four?

Gods, I'm losing track of time. Of space. Of sensation. All I can do is feel him. Suck him. Taste him. Relish his touch.

He nibbles my sensitive nub, shooting me into oblivion without warning and causing me to scream around his dick.

Then I'm screaming into the air.

And suddenly my sounds are muffled by a pillow and my Alpha is behind me, his hardness pressing into my rump while his hand remains against my nape, holding me down.

Oh, Gods… Oh, Gods…

I can feel him stretching me.

It hurts.

It burns.

But it's… it's… different.

I wince as he thrusts inside me, forcing me to take every inch, just like he said I would. Then I moan as his hand reaches around to strum my sensitive nub. I'm already coming again, my body so pent up and ready for him that it's like I'm completely under his command.

And I probably am.

I'm his. Owned. Possessed. Unequivocally claimed.

My heart races in my chest, my legs unsteady. But he holds me to him by cupping my sex, his thumb circling my clit over and over again.

I'm crying from coming so hard. Crying from being without his knot. Crying from the overwhelming pressure building behind me.

All while he's thrusting. Taking. Using me

completely. And I wouldn't have it any other way. My Alpha is taking care of me. Protecting me. Giving me pleasure.

"Gods, you're amazing," he tells me, his praise cocooning me in a cloud of bliss. "You're taking me so well, tesoro. And you look so good like this, with my cock in your ass, your body sweaty and heaving with the effort of our fucking."

He drives home in a harsh movement that has me bouncing beneath him, my lips parting on a moan just as he sends me over the cliff again with a single stroke.

I don't know how he's doing this. He's magical. Or maybe we're magical together.

I don't care.

I just... I just want to *fly*.

And I do. I fly high. Soaring. Living in a euphoric existence. One where I orgasm over and over again while he claims me brutally from behind.

Until he's joining me as well, his seed hot against my insides.

But I don't feel his knot.

No, he's... he's holding it... Massaging it. The hand that was against my core moved at some point so he could hold his knot back.

I whimper, displeased.

But he shushes me mid-groan and keeps coming.

And coming.

And coming.

Until I'm so full I feel like I'm going to burst.

A whine escapes me from the discomfort, and he finally pulls out, then gathers me in his arms as praise and gratitude leave his lips. "You're perfect, Caja. So damn perfect. I've never had anyone take me this well. I swear you were built for me. Created for me to love and cherish. And I will, tesoro. I fucking will until my dying breath."

My tear-stained eyes blur my vision as I try to stare up at him, another whimper escaping me.

Because I need his knot.

And he didn't give it to me.

He promised to reward me. I was good, wasn't I? I... I thought I did what he wanted. I ate the food. I... I...

"Shh," he shushes me again. "I've got you, tesoro. I just need to rinse us off, then I'll knot you against this wall."

I don't understand what he's saying. I'm too distraught. Too lost. Too *needy*.

This is all so foreign to me. My heat. My... my yearnings.

I don't even know who I am here.

"You're mine, Caja," he whispers against my ear. "And I take care of what's mine."

I BARELY REGISTER his hands roaming over me, my mind too lost in a cloud of misery.

He didn't knot me.

I made us a nest.

A beautiful nest.

And he didn't knot me.

I was good.

But he didn't kn—

I come alive as his cock enters me, my legs instantly tightening around his hips. I don't even know when he picked me up, or how I'm covered in water, or when this all happened. Yet suddenly I'm home. Suddenly everything is right again.

I'm full.

He's here.

He's kissing me, demanding that I respond with my tongue.

Stroking me.

Taking me roughly against the wall.

I moan, my arms encircling his neck. And I give in to him entirely. His touch. His mouth. His harsh pace.

It's perfection. Exactly what I want. What I *need*.

He bites down on my lower lip, drawing blood. I follow suit, turning our embrace into a bloody battle of wills.

It's so rough. So animalistic. So intense.

And then his knot shoots out of his shaft, latching inside me and tying us together for eternity once more.

I don't scream… I die.

Or that's what it feels like, anyway.

Because the entire world is black, and I simply exist in a state of ecstasy.

I am pleasure. And pleasure is me.

Until sometime later when I'm wrapped in a fluffy towel and carried back to my nest. *Our* nest.

For the first time in my existence… I have a safe haven. And an Alpha who cares about me.

He holds me in his arms, humming a soft tune, all while combing my hair.

"I don't know who sent you to me, Caja. But I'm going to thank fate every day for this gift. For you." He kisses my forehead. "Now sleep, tesoro. I worked you hard, and you need your rest. I'll knot you again when you wake."

ENRIQUE

A Few Days Later

I run my fingers through Caja's damp hair, watching her as she sleeps.

She doesn't seem to like pillows. Instead, she's using my chest, which is fine by me. If I have it my way, I'll have one hand on her for the rest of our lives.

I fucking love petting her.

Stroking her.

Just *feeling* her.

I purr for her, telling her with my body how content I am with our mating.

It's been a week of nonstop sex. Oh, I've made her eat. But the only way to truly satisfy my hungry Omega was with my cum.

Down her throat.

In her pussy.

Her ass.

Gods, I'm hard again just thinking about it.

I've taken her little body in every way imaginable, and I want to do it all over again.

But she's starting to stir, her estrus subsiding. I noticed it last night when she fell into a deep slumber after sucking my cock like it was her favorite dessert.

She's learned so much in such a short amount of time.

Calling her a natural feels a little cliché—she's an Omega; of course she's a fucking natural—but she really is an excellent little student.

I slide my fingers from her hair to her nape, then massage the tight muscles there.

She's worked hard this week. Been so damn good for me. I have no doubt in my mind that the fates created her just for me to find.

And in the nick of time, too.

I close my eyes as I force thoughts of Carlos to leave my mind. I don't want to entertain the *what would have happened* line of thinking.

It doesn't matter.

She's here with me.

She's mine.

And we're safe.

The latter became clear to me the first time the phone rang asking me what provisions I required for me and Caja. This was in addition to the suite having been fully stocked upon our arrival, as though the caretakers for the building knew we would be arriving at any moment.

Maybe they did.

I haven't left to speak with Xavier or Francesca yet.

But I did hear Elias's arrival six days ago.

As I haven't heard the sound of a leaving jet, I assume he's still here, waiting to speak with me.

My focus has been on Caja and Caja alone.

Today, that'll have to change. At least for a few minutes while I meet with the others. If Caja is feeling up to it, I'll bring her with me. But I'll understand if she needs rest.

She's creating a life inside her, one I can sense even now.

A pup, I marvel, pleased.

I've never entertained the notion of a family before, having always feared accidentally bringing an Omega life into Bariloche Sector.

As an Alpha, I can only breed with an Omega.

And as an Alpha-Omega pair, we can only create one of two offsprings—Alphas or Omegas.

The former would have been a lot of work in Bariloche Sector, primarily because I would have had to teach the Alpha how to play the game without actually enjoying the game.

And the latter… the latter would have required me and my mate to *run*.

Because there's no chance in hell I would allow Carlos to touch my Omega offspring.

Fortunately, that's no longer a concern. I can embrace this life, embrace Caja, embrace *us*.

My lips curl. "A family," I say aloud. "We've created a family, Caja."

She murmurs in response, on the vestiges of awareness.

I run my thumb along her nape, then return my effort to massaging the muscles there. She's going to be sore all over for the next few days. But I'll enjoy kissing away every bruise, laving away all the hurt, and begging for her forgiveness with my mouth against her clit.

Mmm, maybe I'll wake her that way, I muse, gently pulling her off my chest and rolling her to the bed. She started making a nest last night, her parental instincts kicking in as some part of her registered that she's going to be a mother.

I wonder if she's ever had a nest before. A true nest. Given her tentative nature last night, I suspect not.

Will this nest satisfy her, or will she want something different?

I'll ask her when she's fully awake.

To help her along, I kiss her neck, then continue down to her pretty tits.

She moans as I lave her nipples, then hisses when I kiss the mark on her right breast.

She's practically panting when I reach her navel, then comes alive on a scream when I take her swollen clit between my teeth and nibble.

Using my palm on her belly, I push her back down and suck her clit deep into my mouth to roll it with my tongue.

She shouts my name, confirming she's finally surfaced from her estrus.

Then she growls as I flatten my tongue against her abused nub. A fresh wave of slick pours out of her, telling me she's more than ready for another session.

But this one, I want to be gentle.

Loving.

Tender.

A way to thank her for everything she's given me. For being my mate. For being *mine.*

I crawl back up her body, pressing kisses along the way, and settle my cock against her soaking wet core. "Good morning, tesoro," I purr to her as I angle myself to meet her entrance.

She gasps as I fill her in a single thrust, her legs instantly encircling my hips.

"How are you feeling?" I ask conversationally as I move in and out of her.

"Full," she rasps.

"Hmm," I hum, reaching for a water on the nightstand and pressing the straw to her lips. "Drink."

She sputters instead, a moan clawing its way out of her throat as I continue to move.

"Drink, tesoro," I tell her again, my dick slowly sliding out of her before gliding right back in.

She makes a choked sound, one I really enjoy because it reminds me of the first time she sucked my cock. She was a little too vigorous then, but it felt fucking phenomenal.

Caja takes a long drink as I gently pull out of her once more, then arches as I gradually reenter her. "*Enrique.*"

"Caja," I murmur in response, brushing my nose against hers once I'm seated to the hilt inside her. "You feel so fucking good, mi tesoro."

I bury my head against her neck as she drops the drink off the side of the bed. I'll clean it up later. Right now, it's about her. About us. About *this.*

"Kiss me," she whispers, her words representing a request that I'll never deny.

I take her mouth in the next breath while continuing my slow, measured movements below.

She tries to rush me by digging her heels into my ass, but I ignore her silent demand and instead worship her with my mouth and tongue.

Caja claws at my shoulders, her body pressing into mine.

I growl in response, reminding her that I'm in charge here.

She'll get my knot soon.

But not yet.

Not until I've finished cherishing her beautiful mouth. Stroking every inch of her body. Making her burn as hot as she did while in heat.

She moans as my hands move against her sides, pants when I palm her breasts, and jolts when I stroke the mark I left there.

I love it.

I love this.

I'm pretty sure I love her.

Time is irrelevant.

She's my mate now. My everything. And with that, I've given her my heart.

This female has opened up a new meaning of life for me, allowing me to become an Alpha I never thought I could be. *A mated one*.

And she's going to make me a father, too.

She deserves every ounce of my adoration, every beat of my existence.

I demonstrate that with my lips, telling her without words that I am thankful for her, and that I vow to love her for all of time.

She's it for me.

My Omega.

My only mate.

I'll live and breathe for her. Die for her. Protect her. Do anything she fucking wants.

Because that's my purpose now—to serve her.

"Enrique," she breathes, begging me with her voice to fuck her harder. Demanding it with her little nails in my shoulders and her heels against my ass.

I chuckle, loving this torment. Loving her. "You're mine to tease, tesoro."

"*Please.*"

"Mmm…" I do really like that word from her mouth. She's uttered it a lot over the last week. "How bad do you want my knot, Caja?"

She squeezes her cunt around me in demonstration, making me chuckle again. "That bad, hmm?"

Her little responding growl goes straight to my balls.

"I wanted to take this slow," I tell her. "Show you with my body how much you mean to me."

"I don't want slow."

"I can see that," I murmur, brushing my nose with hers. "But you're sore."

"I don't care." She punches her hips up into mine as I'm slowly entering her, forcing me to fill her faster than I intended.

Gods, that's the hottest feeling in the world.

"All right, tesoro," I say, rolling us so I'm on my back and she's on top. "Take what you want."

Her eyes widen. We haven't tried this yet. I've taken her from behind several times. Missionary style. Against a wall in the shower. Bent over the bed. But not with her on top. Not like this.

"Ride me, Caja," I say.

She presses her palms to my chest to sit up.

Then she begins to move.

And fuck if that's not the hottest sight I've ever seen, her tits bouncing with her movements, her body *taking, taking, taking*.

I watch as my cock disappears and reappears with every shift of her hips, her little body barely able to take me in this position.

Her knees skim the mattress rather than rest on it, her smaller form just too tiny for this to be as impactful as she truly wants.

I can see that strain in her features, her frustration over her inability to ride me effectively.

I let her try for a few more minutes, selfishly indulging in the sight of her.

Then I flip her once more and drive forward until she's a screaming, writhing mess beneath me.

She's going to have some fresh bruises on her hips, but her reactions tell me she doesn't care.

So I keep going.

Drilling her hard.

Taking her to that place I know she's addicted to after a week of fucking.

She screams my name over and over, her nails

scraping down my back as I plow into her, driving her over that precipice into pain-induced pleasure, and forcing her to stay there with my knot.

Her body convulses with mine, my bulb attached to her within, holding us together in this orgasmic existence.

Her face is wet with tears, but her lips are pulled up in rapture.

I cup her cheek and kiss her, holding her to me while my seed fills her to completion.

My knot never seems to want to let go, but it eventually begins to subside, and only then does her bliss start to wane, the pain settling in.

She winces, then trembles as another euphoric quake overtakes her being.

I press my lips to hers once more, kissing her through the process, until she's quietly crying beneath me. "I'm sorry, tesoro," I whisper. "I know it hurts."

She shakes her head. "It doesn't."

I frown. "Then why are you crying?"

"Because I can," she tells me. "Because I'm finally safe enough… to cry."

I hug her to me, her words breaking my heart as her sobs punch me in the gut.

My poor little treasure, so strong for so long… I can't even imagine the agony she's kept hidden inside. But I'm going to spend eternity making it right. Showing her how a real Alpha treats his Omega. Worshipping her. Cherishing her. *Loving* her.

"You're mine now," I murmur, my hand on the back

of her head as I cradle her against me. "No one will ever hurt you again, little treasure. No one."

CAJA

I FEEL RAW.

Exposed.

Vulnerable.

Abused.

And so satisfied that I can barely think straight.

It's... it's an exotic combination of sensations, ones that leave me clinging to Enrique for hours on end. Even now, I'm gripping his hand like it's a lifeline. And I suppose it is. We're in a foreign land, filled with strange scents and unfamiliar faces.

Several of those faces are turned our way now as we exit the building. Enrique stands tall, his Alpha strength on full display.

I try to feign a similar confidence at his side but instead rely on my ability to mask emotions instead.

Except, with Enrique, I don't feel like I have to hide.

He broke through some sort of wall inside me, freeing me into the world for the first time. Making me experience life. Embrace my existence. Just... *feel*.

He squeezes my hand, causing me to glance up at him. "It's okay, Caja. No one will touch you."

"I know," I tell him honestly. Because he'll protect me. I'm certain of it. I can feel his need to guard me, his desire to keep me calm, his promise to never leave my side.

All those emotions whirl in our bond like a kiss to my senses.

Just as I'm sure he can feel my unease. My concern with our surroundings. My faith in him to keep me safe.

He's my anchor now.

My Alpha.

My *mate*.

A loud whistle sounds from ahead as a familiar face appears in the crowd. *Elias*.

I blink in surprise, having not expected to see him here.

"Looks like you waited to knot her on the ground," Elias says by way of greeting. "Good job, *Riq*."

Enrique grunts. "You have a strange obsession with my knot, *Lias*."

Elias considers him for a moment. "No, that doesn't work. I'll stick with 'Enrique.'"

"Then I'll stick with 'Elias.'"

He nods. "Good. Anyway, I'm glad to see you both have finally surfaced. It's been a long fucking week, and I'm missing my mate back home."

Enrique dips his chin in understanding, his hand squeezing mine. "I don't think I could survive that long away from Caja."

I smile inside. Because I don't think I would survive that long without him, either.

"I would have gone back earlier had I realized how long the cycle would be," Elias says, palming the back of his neck. "But at least I've learned a lot since being here. It seems Xavier has been grooming his Alphas for an attack on Bariloche Sector, in an effort to save their Omegas. But we—"

"Beat us to the punch," a dominant voice says as a large Alpha with intimidating features parts through the crowd. "Now we just have to figure out how to bring those Omegas home."

Elias nods. "We're working on that. It'll be a slow reintroduction. A few Alphas are going to come back with us to Andorra Sector to start that process."

"You mean with *you*," Xavier interjects. "Enrique still has a choice to make."

Enrique frowns. "What choice?"

"Xavier here has it in his head that you're going to stay here as his second-in-command," Elias explains as he folds his arms over his wide chest. "I told him there's no way you're going to do that when you can have access to my toys in Andorra Sector. But he insists on giving you the choice."

Enrique's frown deepens as he glances at Xavier. "Second-in-command?"

The big man shrugs. "It's an open position, one I think you're well suited for."

"What about Fran and Philippe?"

He snorts. "They insist on being my pack enforcers, and neither of them is interested in leadership."

"Yet you assume I am?"

"From what I've seen, yeah. You're a natural."

Enrique just stares at him. "You've barely seen anything from me. I just got here."

"Yeah, and you're already challenging my decisions and choices. So…" He waves a hand. "Obviously, you're suited for the position."

"Questioning your decision to give me a job without really knowing me doesn't qualify me for a job, Xavier," Enrique argues.

"You punched me," he throws back, stalking toward us. "And you refused to submit."

"Because I wanted to get to my Omega," Enrique grits out. "And you were in my fucking way."

Xavier gestures to his massive form. "Most people don't try to go through me."

"Most people don't try to block me," Enrique counters, the two men almost chest to chest now. "And it was a unique situation."

"One you reacted to without hesitation," Xavier points out. "Just like you're doing now." He looks at Elias. "He's absolutely going to be my second-in-command."

Enrique snorts.

But Elias grins. "Yeah, I'm seeing it."

"Seriously?" Enrique asks him, incredulous.

"Look around," Elias murmurs, causing me to do just that.

And what I find is that everyone in the area has taken several steps back, all of them gaping at Enrique.

Respect and fear seem to be reflected in their wide gazes. Some of them are even bowing their heads.

Enrique curses.

Elias merely grins even wider.

And Xavier nods. "I'm right."

"The fuck you are," Enrique grumbles. "I don't even like you."

"You don't have to like me to be my Second," Xavier points out. "But I'll grow on you as you get to know me."

"I haven't accepted," Enrique snarls at him. "I don't accept."

Xavier shrugs. "Maybe talk to your mate first. We have a lot to offer here. Including a way to help your brother." He starts to turn.

Enrique steps after him, pulling me along with him. "What can you do for my brother?"

Xavier pauses, glancing back over his shoulder. "Oh, now you're suddenly interested?"

"Don't fuck with me, Xavier. What can you do for Joseph?" Enrique demands, his dominance pouring off him in waves.

The other Alpha slowly rotates to face him again, his own dominance battling Enrique's.

I shiver, pressing more firmly into Enrique's side.

He instantly relaxes, his hand releasing mine so he can wrap his arm around me. "Lo siento, pequeño tesoro," he says softly. *I'm sorry, little treasure.*

"Estoy bien," I reply, telling him I'm okay.

Xavier glances between us, then folds his arms over his chest in a manner similar to Elias's. Only Xavier doesn't appear nearly as amused as the other Alpha. "You may have noticed Philippe's lucid state," Xavier says. "Yes?"

Enrique simply dips his chin in response, but I feel the tension trailing along his arm.

"Well, we've developed methods here on the island to help undo Carlos's mindfucks," Xavier tells Enrique. "But it'll require Joseph to come here."

"What about Savi?" my mate asks.

"It would be best for her to stay in Andorra Sector while we evaluate your brother's condition. It might take years to bring him back."

Enrique swallows, his unease prickling our bond as he repeats, "Years."

Xavier gives an affirmative incline of his head. "It's not an easy process. But we know it works."

"While we haven't been able to do anything other than sedate him," Elias adds. "However, we've also only had him for a little over a week."

"What exactly would you do to him?" Enrique asks, still focused on Xavier.

"That's a process I can't explain in a few sentences, nor is it something I want to share right now." He glances at me, making it clear he doesn't want me to hear the process. Probably because he doesn't think I can emotionally handle it. "But Philippe can give you a demonstration, if you're interested in seeing what we do."

Enrique is still studying him intently. "That sounds ominous."

Xavier grunts. "Because it's an intense fucking

process. But it's not like your brother just waltzed into his current state, either. That took years of torture. It's going to take a lot to break him free of it."

My mate says nothing, just continues to stare at Xavier.

Elias clears his throat. "It's your choice, Enrique. Ander and I will understand if you would rather stay on Venom Island. From what I understand, you have some old friends here, too."

Enrique remains quiet, but I can feel him considering his options. He finally looks at me. "Caja would be the only Omega here until the others are able to visit, yes?"

"No," Xavier says, causing Enrique's eyebrows to wing upward before he returns his gaze to the other male. "We have thirteen Omegas under this dome, all of them mated. Now fourteen with Caja."

"How?" Enrique asks.

But Xavier merely smiles.

"Apparently, they've befriended dragon smugglers," Elias mutters. "Something about the rocks in certain mining areas of this island provides for excellent trading. Give a dragon a box of stones in exchange for a few Omegas, and *voilà*. You have Venom Island."

"I never confirmed that," Xavier tells him.

"You didn't have to," Elias bites back. Then he looks at Enrique. "So what's it going to be? Fancy guns or a job?"

"A leadership position that comes with promised assistance in nurturing your brother back to health,"

Xavier clarifies dryly. "And we can trade for guns, should that be something of interest to you."

Elias grunts. "Mine are not tradable."

Xavier shrugs. "Yours are not the only ones available."

"They are one of a kind, though," Elias points out.

"As are other grades and types," Xavier drawls.

Enrique just shakes his head. "I need to talk to my mate."

"Fine, fine," Elias agrees. "But hurry up. I want to go home today."

Enrique nods, then pulls me away.

We walk in silence for a while, Enrique seeming to take in the various structures built into the lagoon-like landscape.

There's a large tower with waterfalls all behind it, streaming down from a mountain.

Glancing up, I see the sheen of glass hovering above it, confusing me greatly.

"It's a dome," he tells me. "I have no idea how they made it, but I'm guessing dragon shifters had something to do with it."

"I've never heard of dragon shifters," I whisper. But then, I wasn't all that familiar with vampires either until Guðrún.

I frown, thinking of her, and then the others.

"Do you think they're okay?" I blurt out, causing Enrique to frown.

"The dragon shifters?"

"No, sorry, the other Omegas. Guðrún, Hel, those

Arctic wolves…" I trail off, swallowing. "They didn't land here, did they?"

He shakes his head. "No, they didn't. And honestly, I don't know. Ander said there's no way to track where they landed, and all the islands are out of X-Clan jurisdiction. We wouldn't even know where to start hunting or whom to work with to begin the hunt."

I shiver. "Oh."

He pulls me close, the two of us pausing on a path near one of the waterfalls. "I'm sorry, Caja. I… I don't know how to help them."

I bite my lip. "I don't know either." And I hate that. I hate that we can't help them.

But this world… it's about survival.

I've known that my entire life.

And I'm certain the other Omegas learned that lesson early on, too.

Enrique pulls me into a hug. "I'm sorry," he repeats.

"It's not your fault."

"It is," he whispers. "I was the Alpha in charge. They were under my protection, and I failed them."

I shake my head. "You didn't purposely crash the jet, Enrique. I would never blame you, or even Hel, for that." I swallow. "If this experience has taught me anything, it's that fate has a plan for all of us. And her plan for me was to bring me to you."

Which suggests her plan for us was to guide us here.

Just as her plan for the other Omegas was to send them to whatever island they landed upon.

"Maybe those islands have secrets," I whisper aloud. "Just like this one seems to." I'm referring to the surprise

I felt in our bond when Xavier spoke about this compound, specifically about being able to help Joseph.

"Maybe," he agrees, resting his chin on my head. "For the other Omegas, I hope you're right."

"I hope I am, too," I tell him, swallowing. "So what do you want to do?" I ask, curious about his thoughts. I think it's pretty obvious that we should stay, but he doesn't seem very keen on remaining here with Xavier.

"I can't help those other Omegas," he says slowly. "But I can help Joseph, and potentially the Omegas mated to the Alphas here."

"By staying," I murmur when he doesn't add that clarifying comment.

"By staying," he echoes.

My chin inclines in understanding. "Then we're staying."

He glances down at me. "As simple as that?"

I shrug. "I have nowhere else I want to go, Enrique. Since you told me my Alpha was dead, all I've ever wanted—all I've ever hoped for—is to be wherever you are."

His eyes search mine. "How could you be so trusting of me from the start?"

"Because you saved me," I tell him.

"Several Alphas saved you, tesoro. I only broke you out of that cage."

I shake my head. "It's not that, Enrique." I palm his cheek. "You saved my heart. My soul. My very spirit. Just by showing me that some Alphas can be kind. You gave me a reason to live. To look forward to a future. To want more than what I thought my existence should be."

It's not something I can easily explain. It's just… an awakening he provoked inside me. A change in the direction of my mind.

"You made me want to breathe again," I whisper. "So yes, it's as simple as that, Enrique. If you want to stay, we'll stay. Because I will forever be by your side."

He leans into my touch, his eyes falling closed. "You're the new beginning I never knew I needed, tesoro," he murmurs. "I was lost before, unsure of where I would even end up after Bariloche Sector settled into dust. And I certainly never thought I would end up here, with you beside me."

I draw my thumb across his sharp cheekbone. "There's nowhere else I would rather be."

"There's nowhere else I would rather be, either," he admits, his dark eyes opening once more. "You're my future now, tesoro. My everything." He presses his palm to my flat belly. "And I'm going to spend our lives proving that to our family."

I go up on my toes to brush a kiss against his lips. "You're already everything I could ever want, Enrique."

His arm circles my lower back as he holds me against him. "Oh, tesoro. I'm going to be so much more. I promise." He kisses me before I can reply, his possessive touch warming me to my very spirit. "To our new existence," he says.

"To our new existence," I agree.

A new life.

A new purpose.

An unexpected… happily-ever-after.

ENRIQUE

Caja and I watch as Elias's jet prepares for takeoff, the roar of the engine springing to life.

We're not the only ones standing out here, observing the takeoff. Nervous energy taunts my senses, the wolves clearly doubtful about this working.

It's not the glass barricade that has them concerned —the jet landed and took off just outside of it—but the barrier that forces all the X-Clan inhabitants to remain here.

"The dragons are not affected by it," Xavier explained a bit ago. "But we are."

"Because it's a barrier meant to keep X-Clan wolves inside. All the islands have their own methods. This one is programmed to recognize X-Clan genetics. So it acts as an invisible net that basically snaps you back if you approach it."

"I know," Xavier muttered. "That's what I'm saying. We can't get through the barrier. So how the fuck are you planning to leave?"

Elias merely grinned. "By tricking the genetic markers."

Xavier appeared doubtful.

Elias simply added, "Trust me."

"That cocky fucker had better know what he's doing," Xavier rumbles from beside me now, his gaze glued to the rocket.

"I told you—their tech is advanced." And I'm pretty sure Ander told him this as well.

"Yet it crash-landed on my island," Xavier points out.

I snort. "Due to a magical electrical storm created by a completely different breed of wolf. That's not on the tech. That's on… something else entirely."

He glances at me. "Fate."

I arch a brow at that word; it's been coming up a lot lately. "Maybe," I hedge, my arm tightening around Caja as I pull her more firmly into my side. She's no longer studying the jet, her eyes on me. "Are you all right, little treasure?" I ask her in Spanish.

She nods. "I was just… thinking."

"Thinking about what?" I ask, staring down at her.

"About how I haven't seen your wolf yet."

I arch a brow. "You want to see my wolf, tesoro?"

"Yes," she whispers. "Please."

I smile. "I think he's pretty eager to see you, too." It's been far too long since my last shift. And the idea of going for a run with my new mate… yeah, that definitely appeals to me. "Want to go exploring after we're done here?"

She nods again. "I would like that."

191

"Me, too," I agree.

"I wouldn't stray too far from the compound," Xavier interjects. "Or consider exploring the mountains under the dome, at least until you learn the lay of the land out here."

Normally, I wouldn't take kindly to someone giving me advice on what to do and what not to do. But I can hear the good intentions in Xavier's tone.

He knows I can take care of myself.

However, Caja... she's vulnerable. Not just as an Omega, but because of the precious life growing inside her. As wolves, everyone can smell that she's pregnant. It doesn't matter what stage she's in; her pheromones are already changing.

"I think we'll stay in the dome for now," I tell him. It's more than big enough to accommodate a long run. Plus, there were some pretty waterfalls that I know caught my mate's eye.

Maybe we can trot out there and find another lagoon.

Or a cave.

Because I really want to knot my Omega against the rocks.

It was something I looked forward to when I left her in that cavern, and I never had a chance to carry out the fantasy.

So we'll create a new one.

The jet rumbles, a countdown likely initiating over the speaker system inside. We're all too far away to hear it, even with our wolf ears.

But the clearance is needed, the jet's power requiring a safe distance.

Xavier is tense, just like everyone else.

Philippe is on that jet, and I've gathered in passing that the two of them have become very close friends.

Francesca walks over to grab Xavier's hand, giving it a little squeeze. I pretend not to notice, particularly when she releases him and he grabs hold of her once more.

It's not uncommon for Alphas to fall for one another. We may be more compatible with Omegas, but that doesn't mean we all mate Omegas.

Caja curls into my side, her palm going to my stomach as the jet shoots upward. I wonder if she's thinking of the jet that brought us here and how it felt to fly in one of those things.

Or maybe she's thinking about the same thing I am —the crash. I'm not concerned about the barrier. If Elias says he can trick it, I believe him. I'm just thinking about the last time I was on a jet like that and how I ended up here.

It feels like months ago.

But it wasn't that long ago at all.

Ander is going to do his best to locate the Omegas on the surrounding islands, and Xavier has offered to send out a few boats for rescue missions, but he can't go much farther than Outcast Island, which is right next door.

Ander told him to hold. He's going to see what information he can gather first.

I'm not hopeful.

I failed those Omegas. I may never forgive myself for it. But Caja helps. She doesn't blame me at all, says it was a freak circumstance of fate.

And there's that word again, I think, glancing down at the female I'm destined to cherish for the rest of my existence.

Fated mates may not be a thing for X-Clan wolves. But it sure as shit feels like we were destined to find each other.

She glances up at me, her big black eyes filled with trust. "Ready to run?" she asks me softly.

I nod and kiss her head.

The jet is nothing but a speck in the sky, the barrier long behind it.

And everyone out here is just... gaping.

Xavier included.

"And now you know Elias's cockiness is warranted," I muse.

Xavier blinks, then swallows, his astonishment clear. But all he says is "I need to call Ander."

And he stalks off toward the compound.

Francesca shakes her head, her lips curling into a smile. "He grows on you."

"Sure," I say, not believing that for a second. "Why aren't you his Second?"

She shrugs. "Because he needs someone who will challenge him, and I'm not cut out for that."

"You used to challenge me all the time," I tell her, incredulous.

Her smile returns. "Yeah, that's different. I like annoying you. But X..." She trails off, her eyes taking on a dreamy look. "I don't challenge X. At least, not like that."

I don't ask for details. But I can imagine what she means.

Caja's nails dig into my shirt a little, drawing my focus back to her. She's looking at Francesca as though she would like to challenge her.

My possessive little Omega.

I decide to help cure her of any jealousy by leaning down and capturing her mouth with mine, not in a sweet, chaste kiss but in a deep, claiming way that leaves no imagination as to how I feel about her.

It serves a purpose of also showing all these unmated Alphas out here that she's mine, not that any of them have dared to look at her. But this will ensure that none of them ever do.

She clings to me in response, moaning as I pull her even tighter against me. I'm already hard, despite over a week of fucking. It's been several hours since I last knotted her. I would happily do it again right now, right here.

But my little mate wants to meet my wolf.

"Let's go for that run," I say against her mouth.

She groans in protest.

"We'll make it a fun game of chase," I add. "And when I catch you, which I will, I'll fuck you."

She shivers, her groan turning into a moan. Her long black lashes flutter as she blinks her eyes up at me. "I think I'll like that."

"Oh, little treasure, I know you will," I tell her, smiling.

Most of the crowd—Francesca included—has backed away from us by the time I turn toward the dome. And it doesn't take us long once we're inside to find a safe place to disrobe for our run.

Caja watches me with a hungry look, her gaze roaming over every inch of my exposed skin. I return the favor in kind, then call upon my beast to take over.

He practically leaps out of my skin, more than ready to officially meet his mate.

She doesn't immediately shift, instead stepping forward to run her fingers through my gray-black fur, her gaze filled with wonder.

"You have hints of silver in your coat," she marvels, dragging her touch up to my all-black muzzle. "Wow." Her touch goes to my black-tipped ears, then down my head to cup my cheek. "You're a very handsome wolf."

My beast makes a sound that I swear translates to "I know," then leans against her hand and closes his eyes.

We stand like that for a long moment, her thumb tracing little circles into my fur.

Then she eventually lets go and allows her own animal to come out to play.

My wolf growls in approval, very pleased with our little mate's sleek black coat and lithe form. And he shows his pleasure by stalking over and giving her a playful nip on the neck. It's a domineering move, but also one that vows protection.

She's ours.

And we are hers.

Forever and always.

Let's run, I think, my wolf grunting in agreement.

But before we can start running, our little mate takes off into the wilderness, making a beeline straight for the waterfall.

My beast's tongue lolls out of the side of his mouth, his gaze sharp and focused as he gives our treasure a head start.

Once she reaches the tree line, we take off.

And the chase to eternity begins...

EPILOGUE

CAJA

A Little Over Three Years Later

"What did I tell you about climbing on the counter?" I say, hands on my hips as I stare down a feisty little Omega pup.

A pup that yips indignantly in response.

"Listen to your mother, little hellion," Enrique murmurs as he enters the kitchen.

Hel—our little hellion—leaps off the counter in response and runs up to put her paws all over Enrique before shifting back into human form.

"Daddy! Daddy!" she chants, making me blow out a breath.

Of course you act like a little angel now, I think, scowling at her.

But one tilt of those little lips has me resigning my anger inside. Because damn it, she really is adorable.

Enrique picks her up to swing her around, his dark

eyes grinning with pride. "Hey, niña," he says, his combined use of languages causing our little monster to start babbling Spanish right back at him.

None of it makes sense yet.

Not really.

However, a few key words stand out, most of them involving *mama* and *reglas*. Mom and rules. Sounds about right.

Sighing, I go back to cleaning up while Enrique tells Hel that there's someone he wants her to meet. I stiffen when I realize who that someone is.

Joseph.

I can smell him now that I'm not consumed with the bleach in my hands.

My gaze goes to Enrique, and there's a question lingering in his depths. *Do you trust me?* he seems to be asking.

Trusting him has never been an issue.

But Joseph... Joseph is an unknown.

Enrique has worked hard with him over the better part of the last three years, only allowing me to visit a handful of times on recent occasions.

And none of those occasions were favorable.

Joseph was never mean or cruel, just disinterested. Like he wanted nothing to do with me. He wouldn't even look at me.

But if Enrique thinks this is the next best step, then I trust his judgment. Because I know what this means to him. And I know how important Hel is in his life. He would never endanger her or me.

So I nod.

He gives me a small smile and cocks his head toward the living area.

Swallowing, I follow him and stand by the couches. They're framed by windows that overlook the waterfalls behind our building—one Enrique chose for us when Xavier gave us the option of where to live on Venom Island.

While we've been here for over three years, sometimes it still feels new.

Now is one of those times.

Maybe because I'm constantly afraid this little bubble of utopia Enrique and I have built together is always at risk of being popped.

But as his brother enters our home, I feel my shoulders relax. Because he's... *smiling.*

I don't think I've ever seen Joseph smile.

"You must be Hel," he says to our little one.

She doesn't respond, instead clinging to her dad like he's her anchor in life.

I understand because I see him as mine, too.

He runs a calming hand down her back. "This is your Uncle Joseph," Enrique murmurs. "Do you recognize his scent? It's kind of like mine."

He also looks like you, I think. They may be fraternal twins, but they have the same dark hair and matching irises. Only Joseph's eyes have a haunted gleam to them that I suspect will never go away.

Hel tilts her head back to sniff the air, her little nose scrunching. "Why?" she asks.

"Why does he smell like me?" Enrique rephrases, ensuring he understands what she's inquiring about.

"Yeah," she says. "Why?"

"Because he's my twin brother," he explains. "You know how Daddy keeps saying he wants Mommy to give you a sister or a brother?"

I narrow my gaze and make sure he can feel my response to that via our bond.

His lips twitch, but he doesn't otherwise acknowledge the *absolutely not* vibrating within me in response to more children.

Not yet, anyway.

Hel is a handful.

Plus, I don't know that my heart can take having another. I love Hel and Enrique so much that I'm not sure there's room for more.

But Enrique is convinced there is.

Fortunately, he's not pressuring me. He's just making sure I know he's very open to creating more pups.

And lots and lots of knotting.

"Yeah," Hel murmurs, answering Enrique's question. "But Momma says no."

"That she does, little hellion. That she does," he muses, winking at me over his shoulder.

"Momma isn't changing her mind either," I reply.

"We'll see," he murmurs.

"No. No, we won't."

He just looks at me with one of those smoldering looks that make my knees weak.

I try to glare at him. But I'm pretty sure it comes across as something else entirely because his nostrils flare in response.

"Do your mommy and daddy do this a lot?" Joseph

asks as he squats down to put himself closer to Hel's level.

She nods jerkily, her little hands still clinging to Enrique.

Joseph nods with her. "It's because they love you very much."

Hel scrunches her little nose. "Yeah?"

"Yep," he tells her. "I can tell by the way your daddy looks at your mommy. It's how I used to look at my mate."

Enrique's shoulders stiffen with Joseph's words, but his brother either doesn't notice or doesn't react to it.

Instead, he cants his head to the side and asks, "So why did they name you Hel?"

Our daughter pinches her lips to the side and looks up at Enrique. "Daddy?"

He joins his brother in the squatting position, but his shoulders remain tight with the movement. "We've told you this story before, little hellion. Do you want to hear it again?"

She bobs her head. "Yeah."

Enrique smiles and stands while picking her up, then moves to sit on the couch.

Hel reaches for me in the process, making it clear she wants me to join.

When I do, she crawls into the space between us and leans her head on my shoulder while Joseph takes a seat on an adjacent chair. His slow movements feel purposeful, like he's thinking through everything before he does it. But as he settles into his seat, he is the epitome of calmness.

If it weren't for the dark torment lingering in his gaze, I would almost believe his facade.

"Mommy and Daddy ended up here because of an Omega named Hel. We believe she played an important role in our being together. So we decided to name our little Omega after her." He cups our daughter's jaw as he speaks and leans down to place a kiss on her head.

"Hel is also a feisty Omega," I add, using the present tense because I know Hel's alive. We haven't spoken. However, Ander discovered through his contact that she was not only found but also very happily mated now. Just like me.

From what he's been able to learn, most of the Omegas survived. Only a few are unaccounted for. Like Guðrún. Although, there have been rumors of a power shift in the vampire nests, and I like to think it has something to do with her.

"What's f-feises?" Hel asks.

"Feisty," I repeat gently. "It means she's strong."

"Just like you," Enrique adds, bopping her on the nose. "And just like your mom."

"Still not giving you a second pup," I tell him. Although, we both know I'm lying. I will someday. Just… not yet.

He chuckles. "Always thinking about my knot, tesoro."

Hel looks up at him. "What's a kah… kah… not?"

His amusement dies. "Something you're never going to learn about."

I snort.

His gaze narrows. "*Never*," he repeats.

I just shrug.

"It's like this," Joseph says, startling me. I'm about to leap out of my chair to stop whatever he's doing when I see he's holding up his shoe. "I struggle with tying my laces, so I knot them."

A breath leaves me on a shudder, my body seeming to disappear into the couch behind me. Because wow. I… I did not expect him to say that. Or to say anything at all.

"Oh." She twists her lips again. "Why?"

"Why is it hard?" he asks, doing what Enrique does when he's trying to find out what Hel is really asking.

She nods. "Yeah. Why?"

"Because my hands shake a lot these days," he tells her softly, his words breaking my heart.

"Why?" she asks.

"Because they do," he replies, shrugging. "Sometimes things happen that we can't explain."

"Oh." She considers that for a moment, then follows up with her favorite question. "Why?"

He laughs a little, the sound a bit rusty in nature. "Magic."

She nods like she understands. Then she looks at Enrique. "What's magic?"

He sighs, giving his brother an exasperated look, then attempts to define the concept for our child.

The conversation goes as expected with a lot of questions from our little wolf. By the time they're done, it's nearly Hel's bedtime, so I take her to her room to begin her routine.

Enrique joins us a bit later to give her a kiss good night, then returns to Joseph in the other room.

Over an hour later, I leave a sleeping Hel and find Joseph talking to Enrique on the balcony outside our dining area. They're deep in conversation, one I don't want to interrupt. So I go get myself ready for bed instead.

"Joseph said to extend his thanks for letting him meet Hel," Enrique tells me as he enters the bathroom, where I'm dressed in a robe. "I think it helped him."

"You do?"

He nods, then he rolls his neck. "He needs… normalcy. Something to get him out of his head."

"Did he go back to his, um, quarters?" I ask carefully, aware that Joseph doesn't live among the others under the dome. He stays in a cabin just outside of it now, which is much better than the padded room he lived in before.

"Yeah," Enrique murmurs. "He needs to pack."

I frown and turn around to face my mate. "Pack?"

He dips his chin again, his gaze catching mine. "He's heading to Andorra Sector tomorrow. To see Savi."

My lips part. "What?" He's refused to see her for months. "He's finally ready?"

Enrique huffs. "No. Not at all. But he needs to do this. He has to see her. Because if his presence won't wake her from that coma, then nothing else will. And then…"

I swallow. "And then…" *The humane thing would be to let her die*, I think, finishing the sentence with a shiver.

He pulls me into his arms, his chin resting on top of my head. "It has to work," he whispers. "It has to."

I nod, agreeing with him.

But I can't help wondering, *What if it doesn't?*

He holds me for a while, no doubt feeling my sadness and concern through our mate bond. Then he pulls me into the bedroom, where he strips me of my robe before removing his own clothes.

"I need to hold you in your nest tonight," he tells me. "Please, tesoro."

"You can always hold me," I murmur. "I'm yours."

"And I'm yours," he echoes, lifting me into his arms to settle us both inside my pillowy haven.

Our pillowy haven. "It's *our* nest, Enrique," I remind him.

"I know. But I like hearing you correct me," he admits, his face in my hair as he holds me close. "Just like I enjoy hearing you deny me."

"We are not discussing a second pup right now," I mutter.

He chuckles. "No. But maybe next week during your heat?"

I growl, making him laugh more.

"I love you, pequeño tesoro," he whispers. "I love you so fucking much."

"Sweet talk won't get you another pup," I mutter, causing him to push me to my back as he towers over me.

"No, my knot will get me another pup," he says. "The sweet talk is just me worshipping my mate."

I roll my eyes. "You're trying to seduce me."

"Always," he admits. "But I value your consent, Caja. You know that, right?"

I do.

He's never forced me to do anything.

Never taken me against my will.

Always ensures my comfort above everything else.

And completes me in every single way.

Because he's my Alpha. My mate. My perfect wolf.

I cup his cheek and smile. "I love you, too," I tell him. "More than I ever thought possible."

And the same goes for our little hellion.

Our Hel.

"You've given me reason to breathe," I murmur. "And for that, I will always be grateful."

"Just as you provided me with a future I never knew I needed," he whispers back to me. "And for that, I will always be yours."

Thank you for reading *Venom Island*!

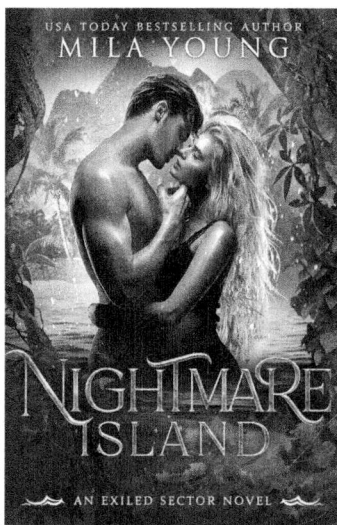

NIGHTMARE ISLAND

Losing my husband broke me, but crash-landing onto Nightmare Island might just kill me.

This isn't just any island.
It's where the feral are sent to die.
The ones with nothing left to lose.
And now, I'm trapped with the most vicious pack shifters alive.

I've survived before—endured a forced marriage.
But this? This is different.
The wild shifters watch me from the shadows
Their glowing eyes track my every move.
Their growls vibrate in the air.

I'm their target.
A prize to be claimed.

Then he finds me.
Ghost.

He says he'll help, but nothing comes without a price.
And he wants more than I'm willing to give.

Just when I think I've hit my limit…
I start to experience my first heat.

The question isn't if I'll survive this place.
It's what I'll become when the fire finally consumes me.

Author's Note: *Nightmare Island is a standalone book and part of the Exiled Sector shared world. These books contain dark themes, Omegaverse vibes, unforgiving men, and the women who defy them. It's a paranormal romance set in the Savage and Shadowlands Sectors world.*

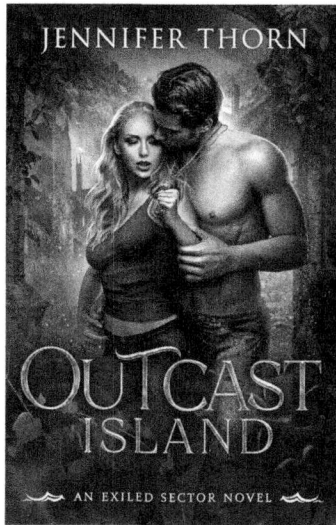

Outcast Island

**They're hunting me.
And I didn't even get a chance to run.
But it doesn't mean I won't *bite*.**

When I was sold into slavery, I made sure I wasn't worth bedding. I bit. I fought. I made such a snarl of things, they drugged me to try and calm me down.

They would have eventually won, had I not been rescued.
Silly me, thinking that was the end of it.
Of course I would crash land on an island.

And now I'm being hunted on this exiled sector of brutal vampires.

They're after my body and my blood.
Magnus is one of them.

I should be terrified of the gorgeous male who has taken
me to his lair. Yet, when the blood has washed off and
the moon turns red from his dark deeds, I realize he's
not like the others.

He's darkly beautiful.
He's patient in his form of hunting me.
He's powerful in the way he says he'll claim me.

But he's waiting for something.
I'm not entirely sure what.
Because I'm not like the females he knows.
There's no way I can go into heat and take his knot like
he wants.
There's no way I can take his seed.

… Right?

Author's Note: *Outcast Island* is a standalone novel in
the Exiled Sector series featuring strong AOB themes,
nesting, growling, purring, breeding, and of course
—knotting.

LEXI C FOSS

USA Today Bestselling Author Lexi C. Foss loves to play in dark worlds, especially the ones that bite. She lives in Chapel Hill, North Carolina with her husband and their furry children. When not writing, she's busy crossing items off her travel bucket list, or chasing eclipses around the globe. She's quirky, consumes way too much coffee, and loves to swim.

Want access to the most up-to-date information for all of Lexi's books? Sign-up for her newsletter here.

Lexi also likes to hang out with readers on Facebook in her exclusive readers group - Join Here.

Where To Find Lexi:
www.LexiCFoss.com

Also by Lexi C. Foss

Blood Alliance Series - Dystopian Paranormal

Chastely Bitten

Royally Bitten

Regally Bitten

Rebel Bitten

Kingly Bitten

Cruelly Bitten

Blood Alliance Standalones - Dystopian Paranormal

Blood Day

Blood City

Crave Me

Frost Bitten

Dark Provenance Series - Paranormal Romance

Heiress of Bael (FREE!)

Daughter of Death

Son of Chaos

Paramour of Sin

Princess of Bael

Captive of Hell

Elemental Fae Academy - Reverse Harem

Book One

Book Two

Book Three

Elemental Fae Queen

Winter Fae Queen

Hell Fae - Reverse Harem

Hell Fae Captive

Hell Fae Warden

Hell Fae Commander

Hell Fae Prince

Hell Fae King

Immortal Curse Series - Paranormal Romance

Book One: Blood Laws

Book Two: Forbidden Bonds

Book Three: Blood Heart

Book Four: Blood Bonds

Book Five: Angel Bonds

Book Six: Blood Seeker

Book Seven: Wicked Bonds

Book Eight: Blood King

Immortal Curse World - Short Stories & Bonus Fun

Elder Bonds

Blood Burden

Assassin Bonds

Mershano Empire Series - Contemporary Romance

Book One: The Prince's Game

Book Two: The Charmer's Gambit

Book Three: The Rebel's Redemption

Midnight Fae Academy - Reverse Harem

Ella's Masquerade

Book One

Book Two

Book Three

Book Four

Netherworld Fae - Reverse Harem

Their Lethal Pet

Bride of Death

Noir Reformatory - Ménage Paranormal Romance

The Beginning

First Offense

Second Offense

Third Offense

Fourth Offense

Underworld Royals Series - Dark Paranormal Romance

Happily Ever Crowned

Happily Ever Bitten

X-Clan Series - Dystopian Paranormal

X-Clan: The Origin

Andorra Sector

X-Clan: The Experiment

Winter's Arrow

Bariloche Sector

Venom Island

V-Clan Series - Dystopian Paranormal

Blood Sector

Night Sector

Eclipse Sector

Vampire Dynasty - Dark Paranormal

Violet Slays

Crossed Fates

Other Books

Scarlet Mark - Standalone Romantic Suspense

Rotanev - Standalone Poseidon Tale

Carnage Island - Standalone Reverse Harem Romance

Monsterland Mayhem - Standalone Reverse Harem Romance

Claim Me - Standalone Reverse Harem Romance

Printed in Great Britain
by Amazon